THE LEVELS

A delight – a funny, painful, beautiful book – Jane Gardam

Benson's strong visual sense conjures up vivid imagery from the heart of the countryside. – Sunday Times

A very apt and unillusioned sort of modern pastoral, blessed with the kind of narrative gift that's like perfect pitch. – The Guardian

A LESSER DEPENDENCY

The lack of adornment lends the novel the directness of a folk tale and sharpens its sting. – The Independent

...touched with poetry. Benson's gift is to capture in strong visual terms the earth-based intuition of those 'dropped in the sand and tuned to the rhythms of tiny island life'. – Sunday Times

THE SHAPE OF CLOUDS

Vividly, defiantly realistic at times, luridly surreal at others, his writing's ability to compound striking metaphors of the abstract with a graphic physicality has won him a deserved following.
– TLS

Beautiful writing and thoughtful language... page after page of stunning prose. – Time Out

THE OTHER OCCUPANT

Restrained, deadpan and unaffected, Peter Benson has one of the most distinctive voices in modern British fiction... a gem of understatement and compassion. – Evening Standard

Layers and crevices, gaps and fissures as important as what is said, all add up to a short novel of power and persuasiveness. – Financial Times

A rare book: compact, exquisitely crafted and intensely upsetting... Benson's cryptic, understated style is ideally suited to the emotive themes which he develops. – Sunday Times

TWO COWS AND A VANFUL OF SMOKE

The real magic of the book is in its evocation of a mystical English countryside... the prose twists and rolls like a vine creeping over a medieval brick wall. – New Statesman

An adventure story written in Benson's distinctive, flourished-filled style and suffused with his deep and abiding love of the West Country. – Daily Mail

THE STROMNESS DINNER

Peter Benson has the miniaturist's eye for the tiny details that bring grand themes alive. His novel is humorous, humane and horrible good (as we say in Stromness.) – Duncan McLean

Benson's snappy novel rattles along with irresistible pace and panache... his story will captivate and entertain and the happy ending is a great treat during the current pandemic nightmare. – Val Hennessy

KIDNAP
FURY OF THE
SMOKING LOVERS

KIDNAP
FURY OF THE
SMOKING LOVERS

PETER BENSON

Seren is the book imprint of
Poetry Wales Press Ltd.
Suite 6, 4 Derwen Road, Bridgend, Wales, CF31 1LH

www.serenbooks.com
facebook.com/SerenBooks
twitter@SerenBooks

ISBN: 9781781726747
Ebook: 9781781726754

The publisher acknowledges the financial assistance of the Books Council
of Wales.

Cover: original artwork by Eilidh Warnock
https://eilidhwarnock.wixsite.com/mysite/

Printed in Bembo by Severnprint Ltd, Gloucester

KIDNAP
FURY OF THE
SMOKING LOVERS

At the time no one understood why a woman like Anne Swaine took off with Fargo Hawkins and drove from Broadstairs in England to a seaside town in North Wales. No one understood but they did wonder. They wondered because Anne and Fargo's lives were reflections of everyone's possibilities and in that year, possibility had been stolen by ghosts. But if ghosts are memories that cannot be quiet then it is our job to raise a fright of the things and lead them by the hand, and show them the flight of their own troubles. For what are their troubles but the tombs of our own confusions, and the beats of change?

The year was 2012. The season was summer. Music drummed and then grew faint. The country was shot and the weather wrong. The air was damp, rain fell every day, puffins drowned in their burrows, butterflies flew into mist, potatoes rotted in their rows. Roads turned into rivers and rivers into lakes, the sea rose and Radar sat on the back seat of the car and made misty patches on the windows.

Radar was the dog who accompanied Anne and Fargo in their flight. With his appalling breath, rheumy eyes and advanced case of alopecia, he was not the most attractive dog to have joined a couple of people on a dash through two damp countries, but he was the most loyal. "Dear Radar", as people who'd given him a pat or bone would recall. "He was lovely, but he'd have your hand for a pork chop."

So there was Anne, Fargo, Radar, a poor car, raging clouds, teeming rain and a butcher, a confused gardener, a pair of wondering sons, some private detectives, a number of people who worked in catering and hospitality, a widowed hotel owner, tarmac and a handful of other things taken from Anne's house. The house was Hyde Hall, and stood in two acres outside Broadstairs in the county of Kent of England, and the taken things included a guide to British wildlife, a penknife, £9,653.45 in cash and a bag of apples. But none of these things mattered, and neither did a tin of travel sweets, a pair of wellington boots, three bottles of red wine and a random selection of tunes. What did matter was the impulse of love and its heat, and the route of its success. Because if the heart is forced to plan so it fails and gives nothing, but when it is allowed to find its own range, it takes a step from the ledge, spreads wings and flies. And at that time of rain and mist and flood, hearts did find their beating place, a pyx for the priests to carry from the mountain to the temple and then, the psalms sung, the sermon said and the service over, back again.

*

Fargo Hawkins had a face like a slapped squirrel, muscles like a boxer's, black hair and a mind like a bowl of macaroni cheese. His hands were the size of a bag of galvanised nails and when he smiled, dimples appeared in his cheeks. He was loyal and strong, and his part-time hobby was drinking. He wasn't stupid but didn't know what was happening after the fourth pint. Every now and again he tried not to have that fourth pint, and most of the time he succeeded. He succeeded because he loved to work and liked to keep busy and didn't like hangovers. When he woke up in the morning, he didn't like to think the spiders in the skirting boards were whispering about him.

The first job he had when he left school was with Thanet District Council's parks department. He stayed with the council for two years, learning about municipal planting, mowing grass, clearing ponds and marking white lines on sports fields. He enjoyed sitting in damp sheds smoking roll-ups, liked the taste of sandwiches that had spent four hours in a plastic box, and loved the smell of petrol mixed with grass cuttings. But he didn't like his bullying boss or the attitude of some people who walked dogs. He'd be getting on with his work, weeding beds, raking grass, picking litter, when some hound would appear and try and hump his leg before taking a dump on a floral clock. So Fargo packed it in and got a job at a fruit and vegetable nursery on the Sandwich Road. This lasted eighteen months – he was made redundant when the owner was declared bankrupt and skipped to Spain.

By the late spring of 2012, he hadn't worked for a couple of months. He was sharing a house in Ramsgate with some people who didn't do a lot, and their not doing a lot had robbed him of ambition, but when he saw an advert for a job at Hyde Hall, "General handyman and gardener required. Live in position." his ambition returned. He liked Broadstairs, and even though he'd once been banned from every pub in the town for pissing from the promenade onto a beach meeting of evangelical Christians, he figured that three years had passed and people would have forgotten the incident, and the publicans who'd barred him would have moved on. Or up. Or sideways. Or whatever publicans do when they spend longer than eighteen months in the same pub. So he phoned the number on the advert and got an interview with Harry Swaine, owner of a chain of butcher's shops and owner of Hyde Hall. A florid man with tiny eyes and pink blotches on his flabby face, he was impressed with Fargo's horticultural experience and gave him the job on the spot. "As long as you can start tomorrow," he wheezed.

"I'll start today," said Fargo.

"Good lad," said Harry, and he went off to adulterate some sausages.

Fargo moved into an attic room in the stable block behind the main house. He owned a motorbike, a suitcase of clothes, a phone and a box of random stuff he'd collected. He was happy with this stuff. He didn't own books, a suit, a fishing rod, a telescope, a small collection of stuffed animals or a guide to the mountain ranges of the world. He put his one saucepan on the stove in the corner of the room, lay down on the bed, laughed at the ceiling and rubbed his hands together.

The job involved working with an old bloke called Bert, although working wasn't the word Bert would have used to describe what he did. Once it had been appropriate but now, forget it. But the old man was a fixture, had worked for the people who owned Hyde Hall before the Swaines, and had worked for the people before them. Sixty years, sixty-five, seventy years? No one knew, and no one cared. A few years ago, Bert's knees had gone on holiday to Norfolk and hadn't come back, but Harry had a sentimental streak and wasn't going to sack him. Besides, Bert's head was full of knowledge, the sort of knowledge you can't replace. For example, he knew that if you planted an apricot tree against a south facing wall in the old walled garden, it would die of a worm disease. And if you try to burn elder wood, you'll be cursed for all time, for Jesus was crucified on a cross made of the stuff, or something.

On his first morning, Fargo met Harry in the stable block yard, stared at the watery sunshine and followed his boss through an arched gateway and onto the gravel driveway that led from the road to the estate and the gothic gables of the main house.

They crunched around the house, across formal lawns, through a walled vegetable garden, past the greenhouses that stood along half the south-facing walls, through the far gate by the dovecote and down to the orchard. Through the orchard, past a pair of duck ponds, through another gate and onto a path that led back towards the house. And as they walked, Harry Swaine pointed at this and that, and talked about the jobs Fargo would be expected to do. And when they got back to the lawns, he said "You can start by fetching a mower from the shed behind the laurel at the far corner of the lawns. Bert'll be up there. He'll show you the ropes."

"Okay," said Fargo, and as he left to find the shed, Harry Swaine thought that he'd made the right decision, and Fargo would turn out to be just the sort of lad the garden needed.

*

An early May breeze lifted the curtains, held them like a bride's hands and laughed at the birds that perched on the groom's wires. The groom wasn't sure if he was doing the right thing. He was confused and already lonely. Every time he looked at his bride she looked so pale. And when she looked at her hands she only saw water through her fingers. She could be about to drown and she wondered. What was it like to drown? Could you ever come back from a place where you could know? And as Mrs Anne Swaine turned in her sleep, her dreams snapped and the groom turned to dust. She opened her eyes and stretched. The room was watered with a pale light, feathered, in its way, by the season. The bride fled and the groom stood. And as she stretched and yawned, and her hair rippled across her pillows, Anne reached across and switched on a radio. She liked to listen to classical music in the morning.

The birds on the wire sang against the music. Leaves rustled in the trees outside the window. Swallows turned in the air, dipped and lifted, and thought of the land they had left a month before. This thought, this ripped heat, left its mark on the window. It was all memory. It was not choice. The swallows saw the sodden green of England, the grey of the channel, the yellow of France, the blue of the Mediterranean, the white of the mountains, the red of the desert, the orange of the desert, the fade of the dunes as they failed towards the jungles, and then the music. The drums and pipes, the twirling of the dancers, the turn of the clouds as they waited for the magicians, and the sea.

What was Anne going to do? Go back to sleep? Get up and have a shower? Listen to the radio? Get up and make some toast? Go back to sleep? Lie awake and stare at the ceiling for half an hour? Fly like a swallow? Drift over a trawling boat and watch the nets sink and fill? She made a decision. She got up, went to the window, pulled the curtains, stretched and looked down at the lawn. A lanky lad with large boots and a big smile was mowing the grass. As she stared at him, he reached the far end of his run, turned the machine and looked up at her.

He saw a yawning woman wearing blue pyjamas with her arms stretched over her head. Her hair was a mess, and even from a distant of fifty yards he could see that her face was drifted with boredom. For a moment he was embarrassed and wasn't sure whether to carry on smiling, wave or turn the mower as if nothing had happened. In the end he turned the mower but missed his step and tripped. As he attempted to pretend that he had meant to trip, he looked up at the window again and the woman was looking at him. He spread his arms as if to say "I know I'm an idiot". She shook her head and then disappeared into the darkness behind the window. She dropped her pyjamas on the floor, went to the bathroom, turned on the shower and listened as the sound of the running water joined the sound of the distant mower and the birds that crowded along the gutters to sing.

He made a good job of mowing the lawn, she made a good job of showering, he sat in the shed and drank a cup of coffee from a flask, she went downstairs, made herself a cup of tea and went outside to sit on the terrace. Radar the dog came from the kitchen, lay down beside her and wondered if he might get a biscuit.

She was sipping her tea as Fargo came round the corner. He was on his way to the walled garden where he was going to help Bert with some weeding.

As he appeared around the corner with a rake in his hand, Radar struggled to his feet, managed a single bark and lay down again. Anne said "You want to be careful."

"Says who?"

"Says your boss's wife," said Anne, "but people call me Anne."

Fargo leant on his rake and gave her a grin. He had good teeth for a man who sometimes forgot to brush them, and wide eyes. They reminded her of something, but she thought she would have to think for ten minutes before remembering what that thing was. "I saw you," he said. "You were looking out the window."

"Was I?" she said.

"You were." He thought about saying something else but bit his bottom lip instead. He drew a drop of blood, licked it away, tasted iron, waited. He liked the taste of iron and he liked the look of Anne. She was wearing something that could have been a dressing gown but wasn't a dressing gown. It was made of silk and patterned with roses and thorns and leaves, and was tied loosely around her waist. She was – he thought – around fifty, but he couldn't be sure about that. She was ripe like a top mango. She trickled and oozed, and her skin was the colour of a cheese he'd eaten somewhere. He'd had a few girlfriends, women who fretted about their weight and their arses and their hair and their jobs. He didn't think Anne had ever fretted about these things. Or if she had, she'd told herself to fret about something else. For although there was sadness in her eyes there was hope there too, and longing. Something was almost lost there, but not.

"You're the new gardener?" she said.

"Yes."

She nodded, sipped her tea and looked him up and down. "What's your name?"

"Fargo."

She laughed, and her face changed. The longing faded, and her eyes widened. "I've never met anyone called Fargo before."

"My Dad was into the wild west. My sister's called Wells."

She laughed and then said "I'm sorry."

"You're not the first to laugh, and you won't be the last." He looked at the dog. "And who's this?"

"Radar."

He reached out a closed hand. Radar smelt it, decided the smell was okay, licked the knuckles and Fargo patted the dog's head. "Good boy," he said. 'What sort is he?"

"A bit of boxer, a bit of sheep dog," said Anne. "A good mix," and she spilt some tea on her foot. "So you've got green fingers?"

"I'm not sure about that." He put them to his nose and sniffed. "Maybe…" He pointed towards the walled garden. "I think Bert's waiting for me."

"I'm sure he is," said Anne. "You'd better hurry along," and with that, he shouldered the rake again and sloped off.

Bert waited for Fargo in a brick shed built into the corner of the garden. He sat in an knackered armchair and drank a cup of sweet tea. A digestive biscuit to dunk in the tea, an ancient cap on his red head, eyebrows like panic in a wire factory, eyes grey and faded, fourteen brown pegs of teeth, a back like a banana; he'd become a part of the chair, a casual passer-by would have had to look twice to spot him. All around were stacks of flower pots, balls of twine, jam jars crammed with useless nails and screws, spades, forks, coils of wire, hoes, crumbs and dust. The shed was lit by a skylight in the roof and a window to the left of the door, so Bert sat in a pool of chiaroscuro, and the surface of his tea reflected shimmers onto the roof and walls.

Fargo appeared in the doorway, dropped his rake and said "Bert?"

Bert stirred, looked up at the lad and nodded.

"The lawn's done. What's next?"

Bert nodded again, put his tea on the floor and hauled himself out of the chair. His knees clicked, and he took a deep, wheezing breath. He thought about something. He looked like the sort of man who had spent a lifetime lost in the bramble of one place, but he had more memories of more places than most people in Broadstairs. He'd fought in France, Burma, London and Glasgow, and been married two times. He had eight children and fifteen grandchildren, and lived in a house that was over two hundred years old. Once, he'd kept a diary, and once he'd drawn in sketch books, but now he'd learnt his lessons. What were Bert's lessons? He looked at Fargo, gave a weak smile, scratched his chin and said "Weeding. And when you've finished the weeding, do some weeding." And then he stood up, walked to the door, pushed into the light and looked at his bicycle. It was old but he loved it. He tested the tyres. They weren't flat. He patted the saddle. It was worn. He rubbed some dirt off the headlamp, pushed it on and headed towards the cabbage patch.

*

For the next few weeks, Fargo settled into his new job, avoided the pub and got early nights. Bert let his memories do the curdling thing that memories do in an old man's head. Anne dreamt of things that were tangible but not quite there. Harry left early every morning to visit one of his branches. He had shops in Whitstable, Herne Bay, Margate, Broadstairs, Ramsgate, Canterbury and Deal. His slogan was "Beat Our Meat", displayed over the counter of each shop and printed on the plastic bags his customers were given to carry their chops home in. If he'd stopped for a moment to list his interests, he would have found that most of them started with the letter M. Money, meat, Mercedes-Benz, marmalade, Mars bars, mince, meat. But he didn't have time to stop. He had driving to do, sausages to check, crossroads to cross without slowing down, and union flags to hang in his windows. The Queen was celebrating her diamond jubilee, and like the lambs he loved to slaughter, he loved the Queen. If he had an ambition, it would be to supply her with a full range of meat products, but if that wasn't possible he'd be happy to supply her with a Christmas goose. Just to know that she and her wonderful family were eating one of his birds would make his life complete.

The people who worked for him, the butchers and their women and boys, tolerated him. He had a temper and his put-downs could stun a mayor, but they were easy enough to ignore, and no one felt they had to watch themselves when his Mercedes S-Class pulled up and he heaved himself out, wobbled across the pavement and pushed his way into the shop. His butchers and their women and boys just put their heads down and carried on with their work, and kept their thoughts to themselves. These were in contrast to the thoughts Anne had when he arrived home every evening. These were thoughts of revulsion, sometimes simple madness.

She was expected to keep the house clean, iron her husband's shirts, dust the ornaments and have a hot meal on the table at seven. But beyond this, she had the day to herself. Once, she'd dreamt of being a professional dancer, but that ambition had faded when she grew too tall. Once, she'd dreamt of travelling the world, but when she discovered she was afraid of flying and suffered from seasickness, she'd turned her mind to gastronomy, and enrolled in a course at Le Cordon Bleu in London. Two years later, armed with her Grand Diplôme, she landed a job as a chef de partie at a restaurant in Canterbury. Two weeks later, she met Harry, and eighteen months later they were married.

The rest of the story followed a predictable course. She was pregnant within the year, and by the time her second son was born, Harry's empire was built, and they were living in Hyde Hall. Now, twenty-five years later, the boys had left home, the house was an echo, and her dreams were like pressed flowers in a book someone gave to a charity shop by mistake. Her days were a dusty luxury of hours, filled now with reading, music and walking. Her favourite writer was Thomas Hardy, her favourite composer was Bach, her favourite singer was Billie Holiday, and she collected postcards of paintings by the French Impressionists. She loved French food, and her favourite walk was with Radar, down the drive from the house, and up to a place on the cliffs where she could stand and watch the sea.

Fargo's favourite walk depended on his mood. Sometimes it was through a pub door, sometimes it was from his bathroom to bed, sometimes it was from a shed to a greenhouse. He liked photographs of polished motorcycles and ate a lot of biscuits and pizza. So the distances between them could be measured in many miles, but during those first two weeks, whenever they met a connection sparked, like the one in a movie where a scientist creates a monster by pulling a switch and watching a bolt of electricity dive between a metal ball and a spike of glass.

*

On the Friday of his first week, Anne asked Fargo to the house for a cup of morning coffee. By the end of the second week, a cup of morning coffee in the kitchen was a regular thing. Bert stayed in the garden shed. He didn't think it was proper to spend more than two minutes at a time with a boss, a boss's wife or any of a boss's other relatives. Bert had his ways of doing things, and they mostly involved string.

The kitchen was large and equipped with class appliances. There was an Italian toaster on the sideboard, an American fridge in a corner, a German oven in a central island and Portuguese tiles on the wall. Radar snoozed on a comfortable rug in a bed beneath the window. Fargo sat at the end of a polished table while Anne made the coffee and took biscuits from a tin. She asked him what he'd been doing. He told her. She spooned the coffee into a cafetière. He watched her. He asked her what she'd been doing. She told him. She'd been reading a book about Wales. "I like castles," she said. A strand of hair fell away from her forehead and covered her eyes. She swept it back. Her fingers were delicate and she wore rings.

"I went there when I was a kid," he said. "We went on holiday at a place called Criccieth. Stayed in a B&B. I can remember the smell, even now. Bacon. There's a great castle there and a beach and a famous ice cream shop..." He took a biscuit and stirred his coffee. He liked coffee and he liked it strong. She leant over the table. She was wearing a white blouse. He stared at her and their eyes met. She was embarrassed, he wasn't embarrassed, the crackle in the air was the crackle you'd expect, and they heard it.

It didn't take them long. Two days later, a storm blew through the county. Rain sheeted through the garden, wind ripped the leaves from the orchard trees. When Fargo went out to start work, he found Bert in the shed, doing stuff with plastic netting. He took a wheelbarrow and rake, and went to tidy some fallen twigs and leaves from the lawn. It was June but felt like autumn. The smell of smoke should have been in the air, and the smell of a compost heap.

Harry was spending the day in Whitstable. Anne waited for him to leave the house, listened as the car crunched up the drive and took the road, then lay in bed for an hour, reading a book about someone who walked around the coast of Ireland. It was one of those travel books that says more about the person who wrote it than the subject, and when she got to a chapter that focused on the writer's relationship with stone walls, she closed it, dropped it on the floor and went to the window.

She watched the rain as it ran down the glass, and listened to the wind as it blew across the tops of the chimney pots. She heard a knocking and looked at the time. It was 10.30. She took a dressing gown from the back of the door, slipped it over her shoulders, tied it at her waist and went downstairs.

Fargo was standing on the step, drenched. "Get in here," she said, and went to fetch a towel from the airing cupboard.

"Thanks," he said stepping into the kitchen.

He started drying his hair, she put the kettle on, he sneezed, she took down two mugs, he pulled at his damp shirt and said "Mind if I take this off?" she said "No," and watched as he undid the buttons.

Harry was a fat man. His skin was pale and loose, hung off him like tripe and smelt of vinegar. Fargo's skin was tight and smelt of tar. He sat to drink his coffee at the kitchen table, with his shirt hanging off the back of the chair and the towel around his shoulders. She watched as little drops of water dripped off his ends of his hair and pooled on the floor. She said "Can't Bert find you something to do inside?"

"There's stuff to do in the greenhouse," he said. The coffee was hot. She put a plate of biscuits on the table. He picked a ginger nut, the king of biscuits. As she moved from her chair to the cupboard and back again, he scratched his chin and watched her.

He liked the sound of her breathing. She sounded like a cooling train in a station. He tried to remember something someone had said to him about older women, but he couldn't.

"Another biscuit?" she said.

"Thanks."

"More coffee?"

He nodded.

She poured.

He sipped some coffee and looked at a stack of books on the table. "You like reading?" he said.

She laughed.

He frowned.

"Sorry," she said. "I love reading. Books are my life. What about you? Are you reading something at the moment?"

He thought about the Haynes manual he had in his room, almost said something about it, changed his mind, remembered the last real book he'd read and said "Robin Hood".

"Robin Hood." She nodded at the thought. "Who's it by?"

He didn't know. He thought it was in a comic, but maybe it wasn't. He said "I don't know. I just liked the story. You know, stealing from the rich, giving to the poor. That sort of thing. When I was at home, I used to watch it on the telly."

"And where was that?"

"In the corner of the front room."

"No, silly. Where was home?"

"St Austell. Cornwall. My old man used to work in the clay."

"The clay?"

"China clay. He used to drive the dumper trucks."

"Used to?"

"He was killed when I was a kid. Dumper rolled over him."

"I'm sorry."

Fargo shrugged. "It was a long time ago. I still think about him, but there's not a lot I can do about it."

"And your Mum?"

"She died a couple of years ago."

"So you're on your own?"

"I've got a sister. Lives in Manchester with her bloke."

"You see her?"

"Not for a while. We don't have a lot to say."

Anne ran her finger around the rim of her coffee mug and made a little whistling sound through her teeth. "Sometimes…" she said, and she let the word hang in the air, watched it twist and fade, listened to its echo bounce, wished she hadn't said it, wished she'd said more, went to the sink and poured the dregs of her coffee away. Fargo stood up, took his shirt off the back of the chair, joined her at the sink, put his mug on the draining board and slipped the towel off his shoulder.

"Thanks for the coffee," he said.

She took the towel. Their fingers touched. He turned to leave. She reached out and put her hand on his arm. He looked at her. Her eyes were big and wondering, and he thought that if he reached out and put a hand on her dressing gown she would tip her head back and show him her neck. She reached up her other hand and touched the side of her face. He moved closer and said "You smell great".

"Thanks."

"Really great."

"I go… I go to a special shop. This is the perfume Marie Antoinette used to wear."

"Who?"

"The Queen of France."

They were whispering.

"Why doesn't she wear it any more?"

"Because she's dead."

"What happened to her?"

"You don't know?"

"I left school when I was fifteen. I was a kid. I had better things to do with my time."

"I bet you did," Anne said, and she watched as the rain lashed the window. Somewhere – maybe a mile away – thunder rolled over the sea and slapped against the cliffs. "The sort of things I should have been doing…"

"And what does that mean?"

"What do you think it means, Fargo?"

"I don't know." She squeezed his arm. "Doing stuff?"

A squall rattled the back door. It made her jump. Fargo wasn't nervous. She moved closer. He put an arm around her, pulled her closer and stood like this for a moment. "I feel safe," she said. "I feel safe with you."

"You smell even better like this," he said, and he dropped his hand and let it rest on her waist. She made a sound like a cat by a fire. She made a little movement with her hips that told him it was okay to do whatever he liked, so he did.

The storm blew for the rest of the morning and half the afternoon, wailing at the house, blasting draughts under the door and through the cracks in the windows, rattling the glass, blowing dust down the corridors, frightening birds, lifting slates and flipping them onto paths. Some of the paths were green and some of them were grey, and some of them led through gardens and woods and rain.

Fargo and Anne fed on the paths and met at crossroads, made a pact, returned with a song, played the song, burned the song and placed the ashes in a bottle. The bottle was clear and the message bright and when, after a couple of hours, the phone rang and the spell cracked, she nudged him off the bed, answered the call and said "Yes dear… not a lot…" as he pulled his shirt on and headed for the door. A black, old door. He waited there for a moment and watched her talking to Harry, nodding her head and running her fingers through her hair. The watery light spread from the windows and cut bars across the floor and the bed and her body. She reached up and pulled the sheet up. He smiled and she smiled back and then waved him away. A minute later he was outside again, dashing through the rain towards the greenhouse and Bert who had finished doing things with netting and was now sorting lengths of string, coiling them and hanging them from nails.

He spent the rest of the day dodging the rain, sorting plants in the greenhouse, wiping his face, tipping his head, cleaning seed trays and stacking them in a shed, watching the windows of the house, wondering what he was going to have for dinner, whistling through his teeth and listening to Bert tell him a story about a jackdaw he used to keep as a pet. "Fell out of the nest so I took him home. Used to sit on my shoulder and chatter in my ear. I called him Fred…" and at half past five he went to his room, washed his hands and made some cheese on toast. He was eating as Harry returned from Whitstable.

The rain had begun to ease and the sky had lightened, and once he'd parked his car in the garage, he knocked on Fargo's door and called up at the window.

"Hey? You home?"

Fargo froze. He'd heard the stories. Men who can smell their wives on another man or sense a look in another man's eyes. It's an instinct, something shot from way back when people lived in huts and hunted in forests with sticks and pits. Fargo went to the window, opened it, looked down and said "Er… hello Mr Swaine…"

KIDNAP FURY OF THE SMOKING LOVERS

"Fargo. Good. Got a job for you tomorrow."

"Okay…"

"Mrs Swaine…" he said, and now Fargo felt his legs go at the knees and the blood rush to his cheek. "…wants to visit a garden centre. She'll need a hand carrying stuff."

"Okay…"

"She'll come and find you in the morning."

"Right."

"And make sure she buys you a cup of tea," he said.

"Okay," said Fargo. The blood was still in his cheeks and his knees were still bad.

"Good lad," he said, and waved a hand and went to the house for his dinner. A couple of pork chops, a heap of potatoes, carrots, peas and gravy. Fargo stood and stared at the man's back, watched it disappear, reached out to close the window but decided he needed the fresh air so left it open. The fresh air was good, and so was the thought of the pub. And the sun came out for a moment and hung over the orchard beyond the garden as a cloud passed over its face, and a flight of crows headed for their roost. Before they'd passed, Fargo had grabbed his jacket and was down the stairs from his room, out of the door and walking into town.

*

He went to a pub by the harbour. He didn't recognise the landlord and the landlord didn't recognise him, so he bought a pint and sat outside to drink. A few tourists were enjoying the watery sun and some locals were arguing about fish. A kid was flying a kite on the beach, clouds were flying in a bleeding sky and the smell of seaweed poached the air.

As he sat and drank, Fargo went through the day in his head and thought about what he was going to do.

He had choices and he counted them. He could stay at Hyde Hall or he could jack it in and go back to Ramsgate, Norfolk, Cornwall, Wales or wherever else he thought he could get work, which was pretty much anywhere. But the job at Hyde Hall was a good job and he liked the place. It was as ripe as a pear on a hot windowsill.

He finished his pint, went for another and tried to remember when he'd been so lucky. He carried his drink to the end of the pub's terrace, leant against a wall and looked at the beach and the kid with the kite, and the boats in the harbour.

He liked boats, the shape of their hulls, the comfort he imagined behind their portholes, and the potential for escape in their flappy sails and dirty engines. He didn't know why he wanted to escape or what he wanted to escape from, or even if escape was the right word. Maybe the word was flight. Or run. Whatever the word was, he'd had the thought since his first day in school, when he was five. The idea that he had to get out of this, get away from that, run towards something he couldn't identify but knew was there.

Was this something a place, a person, a feeling, a song or a postcard from his Mum? He didn't know. Maybe it wasn't the idea of escape, maybe he simply needed to keep moving. Maybe he wasn't meant to stay in one place longer than a couple of weeks. Maybe he had gypsy blood. He looked at his pint. Maybe he only thought like this when he drank. He finished it and went to get another.

He tried to imagine his future. This was something he didn't usually do, not because he didn't think he had one, but because he couldn't. But the drink made him do all sorts of things he didn't usually do. Maybe, in the future, he would stop drinking and smoke weed instead. Or maybe he'd sell his bike and buy a plane ticket to America, and get a job in a park where the redwoods grow. Or maybe he'd meet a nice girl, settle down, have kids, live for fifty more years and turn into Bert. There were so many choices and so many futures, and so far to go.

He watched as a gang of locals came and stood at the wall beyond the terrace. They were loud and happy, and as he listened to them talk, he wondered if his mum and dad had ever wondered about their future. When the family had been a real family, in the days when they lived in St Austell, in the days when his dad had left for work every morning at 7.30 and his mum had packed him and his sister off to school and then gone to work in the newsagents on the corner, had she stood behind the counter with her hands dirty from newsprint and copper and wondered what it would be like to hitch-hike from Cornwall to Spain? And had his dad ever dreamt of going to live in Greece, buying a fishing boat and living off sardines? Fargo remembered the time – he was six years old and it was about six months before a dumper had rolled over and killed him – when the family had gone to Falmouth for the day. While his mum and sister went to look at the shops, his dad had borrowed an open boat from someone who worked at the clay pits, and the two of them had taken it out into the estuary. They'd headed through the moorings towards St Anthony Head, and as Fargo steered through the swell, his dad had let out a line of feathers to catch mackerel.

The sun was warm and a breeze was blowing, and as they motored and fished, his dad pointed to the tight sails of a distant boat and said "That's mine."

At the time, Fargo hadn't understood. He couldn't remember being told that his dad owned a real boat, and if he did, why had he borrowed this one? But later he knew what the words meant – it was his in his dreams, and the dreams were dreams of packing a bag of clothes and sailing over a horizon he'd seen but never reached. His own escape. Maybe the idea was in the blood.

His dad was a quiet man, but Fargo had never had the chance to discover what hid behind the silence. The clay pits and the rolling dumper came between the boy and whatever wisdom was ready to escape. For as they bobbed across the Cornish estuary and his dad hauled the first line of mackerel into the boat, knocked the fish into a bucket and watched them thrash to death, he said nothing, just did the job and then played the line out again. And when he sat back and watched Fargo steer and smiled at the other boats and the sea, he gave nothing away. Maybe there was something in his eyes or the way a little smile sneaked onto his face, but if there was, the boy had no idea what it meant.

He knew it wasn't a good idea but as he let the memories sink he went for a fourth pint, and as he drank he felt the kick of whatever it was that made his head turn. The gang of locals had drifted away, the sun was failing, clouds were building in the west, the boats were pretty. A couple of fishing boats were tied against the breakwater, and some pleasure boats were moored in the centre of the harbour. A couple of dinghies were bobbing, secured by long lines that ran from their bows to rings in the wall. He started to walk towards them, the pint in his hand, the alcohol tying a knot in his head. He felt it go one way and then the other, turning tighter and tighter. And when he reached the breakwater, he leant against a wall, finished the drink, felt the knot pinch, tossed the glass into a bin and went to sit by a ladder that dropped into the water.

He'd already made the decision, but it took him a minute to do something about it. He looked this way and he looked that way. The place was quiet. A couple of tourists were wandering along the breakwater, and stopped to look at the old steps and the view of the town. Lights were coming on. Gulls were crying. Rigging was snapping. He smiled. Anyone who looked at him would assume he was a fisherman, the owner of a boat, a man who spent his days watching his step and the weather. He looked like he was meant to be there, like he knew what he was doing. He looked around again, picked up a rope that dropped to a little clinker tender, untied it, turned his back to the water, and climbed down the ladder.

When he reached the bottom, he pulled the boat towards him, steadied it with one foot and climbed in. He untied the rope, let it drop, picked up an oar, pushed it against the wall, picked up the other oar, dropped both into the rowlocks, turned the boat and started to row towards the open sea.

No one came running, no one shouted and waved their arms, and he rowed quickly. A couple of minutes later he was past the end of the harbour wall and into the bay, and rougher water twitched beneath the boat, and rocked it away.

What was he thinking? Where was he going? Did he have a plan? If he asked any of these questions, or if coherent thoughts formed in his mind, they didn't stay there. They faded as quickly as they came, and he turned the dinghy towards the south, France, the Bay of Biscay, Spain, the coasts of Portugal and Morocco, Mauritania, Senegal and West Africa.

He was strong and wasn't bothered when the clouds filled and darkened, and the sea started to chop. He didn't know anything about the tide but he felt the current pulling him east, tugging against his rowing and taking him away. Still he wasn't troubled, and when a wave broke over the bow and splashed his back, he laughed, tipped his head back and licked the salt off his face.

This was escape, and when rain started to fall it could have been adventure. Distant thunder rolled, a pair of gulls came and circled over the stern, and as he watched them turn and swoop, he wished himself into their heads. He wanted to be a bird, he wanted sky. He looked over the side. He wanted to be a fish, he wanted depth. He looked at his feet. His boots were soaked but they could take him anywhere. He looked at his hands on the oars, and the oars as they dipped and rose, and the gulls swooped again, and the rain grew heavier.

Now he started to feel cold, and when he looked over his shoulder and saw lightning flash through the clouds, he decided to turn the boat around. He lifted the left oar and pulled on the right, but as he did a wave broke over the side, one of them popped out of the rowlock, flipped sideways and fell into the sea. He leant over to try and grab it but it was gone, another wave broke, and another, and now he was scared. The top of the alcoholic courage had fallen off, the single oar felt too heavy, and the harbour was fading into the dark and distance. He yelled at the sky and the gulls and himself, and turned in the boat and tried to use the oar to paddle and steer back towards the harbour.

This worked for a few minutes, but then the current started to pull the boat towards the shore. The surf was breaking and as it smashed on the beach and pulled the pebbles, it wailed and roared, and threw up spume that joined the rain and wind. Fargo pulled the oar out of the water, dropped it into the boat, moved to the middle of the boat, grabbed the gunwales and watched as the bow dipped into a wave, was lifted, dropped back and started to turn on its axis. There was nothing he could do but shout again as the next wave took the boat and accelerated it first sideways, then bow first towards the beach and the concrete steps and promenade that curved beneath the cliffs.

A moment later the boat grounded, the stern lifted and Fargo was thrown into the air. He landed sideways and looked up to watch the oar cartwheel over his head, and the side of the boat twisted towards him. He covered his head with his arms, took a blow to his shoulder, grabbed at the beach, turned on his side and the boat was tossed up and flipped over.

Now the alcohol had faded, sense returned, and adrenaline. The boat was a good boat, someone else's boat, and it was lying half in the water and half on the beach. He grabbed its bow and pulled, hauled as far as he could, sat down, stood up, and hauled again, heaving it over the tide line while the rain teemed and the thunder rolled. He tied its painter around a metal ring, climbed the steps to the promenade, and then up another flight to the grassy cliff top. He found a bench and sat down for a moment, stared out at the storm and the sea, and shook his head at himself. What had he told himself, once, twice, three hundred times? Never drink more than three pints. You know it makes sense. And never think you can do something you've never done before. That's so obvious, but sometimes the obvious is so complicated.

*

Fargo woke with an aching head, a bruise on his shoulder, gashes on his arms and hands and a cut over his eye. He showered and stood in front of a mirror and tried to remember what he'd done. It wasn't easy. There was the pub, the locals, the drink and another drink. A walk to look at the boats and then things got blurry. Water was there somewhere, and a ladder. Waves and wind, and rain, and more wind. Rope? He thought there was rope somewhere, but he couldn't be sure.

He dressed slowly, and as he was eating a bowl of cereal he heard a car start up and drive away. Ten minutes later, as he was trying to put on his work boots, he heard Anne climbing the stairs to his room and remembered. She knocked on the door. He opened it, said "Garden centre, is it?" but Anne didn't answer or ask to be let in. She pushed past him and leant against the table. She had a bruise on her face, and her cheeks were wet.

"What happened?" he said.

"What do you think?"

"Did he do that?"

She nodded and looked at him. "And what happened to you?"

He shrugged. "Not sure."

"I went to the pub. Fell over... I'll be okay. But you... Why?"

"He doesn't need an excuse." She reached towards his face. "You sure you're okay?"

Fargo nodded and said "Fucker. Does he know about us?"

"You wouldn't be standing here if he did. No. You're nothing to do with it. He had a few drinks. That's all it takes." She touched her face and winced. "Actually, it doesn't take a few drinks. All it takes is for him to think 'Yeah, maybe I'll give her a kicking tonight.'"

"You should get out of here."

"Very funny."

"What's funny about it?"

She looked at him. Her eyes narrowed and her mouth pinched, and he thought she looked ten years older than she was. Or fifteen. "How the hell could I ever get out of here?"

"You get in a car and drive."

Now she laughed, but it wasn't the sort of laugh that would make another person join in. "Yeah, that's going to happen."

"It could."

"How?"

"You've got a car?"

"The Toyota's mine."

"I can drive."

"And what's that supposed to mean?"

"You know what it's supposed to mean. You got the keys to the garage?"

"Of course?"

"Fetch them."

"Are you serious?"

"Do I look like I'm joking?"

Now Anne looked at Fargo, took his chin in her hand and said "What are you talking about?"

"You know what I'm talking about."

"I need you to tell me. I don't make decisions. I haven't made one for years. I don't know how to…"

"I don't believe you."

"You can believe what you want, but it's true." She looked at the floor. "Okay, maybe sometimes I decide what to have for dinner, but that's about it…" She moved towards him, put a hand on his waist and rested her head on his shoulder. He took a deep breath, put his left hand on the back of her head and turned at the sound of a car. It was being driven fast up the drive, and when it reached the courtyard below Fargo's window, it slewed to a halt and Harry got out.

"No…" she said.

"Shit…" he said as he watched the man storm across the yard. He was red and sweaty, and looked like he was about to have a heart attack.

He disappeared around the corner, went in the front door, stood in the hallway and shouted "Anne", opened the kitchen door and shouted, stood at the bottom of the stairs and shouted, climbed the stairs and stuck his head around the bedroom door and shouted, kicked the bathroom door and shouted some more. When he got no reply, he turned and stood on the landing, scratched his head and let his mind wonder.

She'd deserved the smack. He'd expected his usual breakfast. Sausage, bacon, eggs, fried bread. Beans. She'd told him that if he wanted it he could cook it himself. She'd never said anything like that to him before. Ever. Never. "Anne!' She'd be nothing without him. A hairdresser in a hairdressing shop in hair alley. A cleaner in a house like the house he let her live in. A woman in a greengrocer's shop, bagging apples and spuds. "Anne!" She'd be living nowhere. But she was living here and she didn't have to do anything but what he told her to do. What was the problem? How difficult was it?

Back in the attic room, Anne said "Stay here," she went down the stairs. Fargo said "I'm not going anywhere," and as the downstairs door closed, he went to the window and watched her cross the yard. A moment later, Harry stepped out of the back door. The man looked up at Fargo's window and then looked at his wife. He stepped back from the window, but not before the man had raised his hand and pointed and mouthed a single word. A moment later, he heard a shout and a scream, and when he went back to the window, he saw Harry slap Anne in the face, grab her arm and pull her across the yard.

She struggled so he hit her again, and as he did she fell. He put some weight behind his slaps. "Get up!" he yelled, and he took a fresh grip, yanked her towards him and twisted her head up. "Get the fuck up, get in my kitchen and cook me breakfast!"

Fargo took the stairs two at a time, kicked the door open and stepped into the yard. He took two more steps and stopped. Harry let go of Anne's arm and she dropped onto the cobbles. She took a heaving breath. He looked at Fargo, tilted his head, narrowed his eyes, said "And is this trouble or lover boy? Or both?" and rubbed his hands together. Fargo looked at Anne, watched as a trickle of blood came from her nose and spread across her lips, and a rage popped his head. He looked to the left, looked to the right, saw a garden rake leaning against the stable wall, picked it up, weighed it in his hand and said "You need to pick on someone your own size."

Harry stared at the rake for a moment, shook his head, then patted his belly and laughed. "I don't need to do anything," he said, and he stepped over his wife and walked towards Fargo, who raised the rake and adjusted his grip on the handle. "But you do."

"Why?"

"You're already out of a job and a place to live, but have a go with that and I'll have the cops on you faster than you can pack a bag."

"Is that a promise?"

"Oh yes."

"Then I'd better make it count," and Fargo took a couple of quick steps and swung at Harry's head.

He was quick for a fat man, and ducked as the rake swished over his head. Anne screamed and scrabbled towards the back door, and Fargo took another swing, this time at the legs. He caught him a good one below the knee, and as Harry fell, he let out a low groan. He broke his fall with his right hand, tried to keep his balance but his weight was too much. Fargo took another step and smashed the rake into the side of the man's face.

You could say Fargo was lucky. If Harry had dropped his head or twisted it to the side, or rolled over, the rake would have caught him under the chin, and the tines would have punctured his skin, pierced the thick veins and blood would have fountained. His face would have moved from shock to quizzical, and as he slumped, he would have made a sound between a laugh and gasp, a sort of "urghhaa…" Fargo would have dropped the rake and whispered

"Shit…" Anne would have stood up, staggered and dropped to her knees. Fargo would have put his hands on the man's neck and tried to do something like he'd seen people do in films, but the blood wouldn't have stopped, it would have pulsed through his fingers and pooled across the yard. He'd have said "Shit," again, and Anne would have stood again, turned and ran into the house. She'd have come back with a towel and while the blood turned from a pool into a lake, she would have pressed it against Harry's neck. He would have looked up at her and his lips would have moved and then his eyes would have closed, his head would have dropped and he would have been dead.

And Fargo was lucky. Harry's head was hard. The rake glanced off it, a little trickle of blood came, and before Fargo had a chance to take another swipe, the man had grabbed his ankle and pulled him to the ground. He pulled the rake away and it clattered across the yard. Then he was up and standing over Fargo, and he kicked him in the stomach. As the boy doubled up, Anne screamed, ran from the back door and threw herself on Harry's back. She dug her fingers into his cheeks but before she get a good hold, he started turning. She slapped his head, he laughed, she beat his back with her fists, he laughed some more, he turned faster until the motion made her loosen her grip, then he stopped and she flew off his back and landed in the heap next to Fargo. Harry took a step back, wiped the blood from his face and said "Nice. Very nice…"

Fargo groaned.

Anne made a whimpering sound, like a cat in a fridge.

Harry picked the rake up, walked over to Fargo, pushed it into the boy's stomach and said "You've got five minutes to get out of here."

"Five minutes?"

"Four minutes and forty-five seconds."

"So you won't be wanting me to take your wife to the garden centre?"

Harry rolled his eyes. "Are you trying to be funny?"

"No. Just asking a question."

Harry pushed the rake again, then turned to Anne. "You've got breakfast to cook," and he reached down, took her arm and hauled her towards the back door. Fargo wiped his face, and as the Swaines disappeared into the house, he hauled himself up, went back up to the attic room and pulled his bag out from under the bed.

*

Fargo went back to the house in Ramsgate where he used to rent. The people who lived there laughed when he knocked on the door and said they'd been running a book on how long it would be before he returned. He told them to fuck off and leave him alone. They said "that's gratitude" and went to smoke some weed, laugh at the floor and toss balls of paper into cups. He went to his old room, lay on the bed and stared at the ceiling. There was a water stain on the ceiling, and the window rattled in the wind. The carpet smelt of mice. He closed his eyes.

He'd lasted less than two weeks at Hyde Hall. He owned a motorbike. His parents were dead. He was 21 years old. His head hurt. He was covered in bruises and cuts. He had £235.78 in the bank. He didn't have a single person he could call a best friend. He didn't know French and he didn't know how to play a musical instrument. He didn't know how to cook an omelette. He liked cheese on toast and one day he'd go to France.

He thought about France and cheese and boats, and he thought about Anne. He thought about the way her eyes widened after she asked a question, and the way she flicked her hair out of her eyes when she wanted something. The way she said intelligent stuff but didn't care if he didn't know what she was on about. The little gasps she made when she was excited, and the fact that she knew what all the different types of pasta were called.

So? So she might be able to recognise birds in their flight and fish on a slab, but it was probably a good idea to forget her and move on. A good idea and the best one but he couldn't, and that first night back in Ramsgate he woke up in the middle of the night with a bad feeling. Something wasn't right and the feeling nagged him all the next day. It nagged and pulled, took hold of his sleeve and would not let go, so the following evening he rode to Broadstairs, left the bike in a hedge and sat to watch Hyde Hall. He saw lights and movement behind closed curtains, but didn't see anyone until about half eight. Then Harry came from the front door, locked it, climbed into his car and drove slowly down the drive, out of the gate and turned right. Fargo ducked behind a wall as the headlights swung, and when the sound of the engine had faded into the dark, he jumped out and jogged up the drive to the front door. He hesitated then rang the bell. He heard it echo through the house and a moment later he heard the sound of footsteps. A hand on the doorknob and Anne called out "Who's there?"

He whispered. "It's me."

"Who?"

"Fargo."

A beat. A key turned in the lock, the door opened, Anne said "Quickly…" and he stepped inside. She was in her dressing gown. Her hair was a mess. She'd been crying. "Are you mad?"

"No."

"Then what are you doing here?"

"I wanted to know that you're okay."

She looked at him, held his gaze for a moment and then turned and walked down the hall towards the kitchen. He followed. A bottle of wine was on the table, and a single glass. "What do you think?"

"I don't know."

"Imagine the worst, double it…"

"Has he hit you again?"

"A couple of times."

"Where is he now?"

"Down the pub. But if none of his mates are there he won't stay." She looked over her shoulder towards the window. "He could be back any minute."

Fargo shrugged.

"Really."

"Leave him." Fargo hadn't planned for the words to come out so quickly. He'd planned to talk and lead up to the idea gently, but he couldn't stop himself. He put his hands on her shoulders and turned her to look at him and said it again. "Leave him."

"And do what?"

"Come with me."

Now she laughed. "And where are we going to go?"

He shrugged. "Wales."

"Wales? And what are we going to do in Wales?"

"I don't know. But I know a place."

She laughed louder. "You know a place? What sort of place?"

"It's a town."

"You know a town in Wales?"

"Yes. I told you. Criccieth. It's got a castle and a beach…"

"And a great ice cream shop?"

"Yeah."

Anne shook her head. "You've got so much to learn. Too much."

"If you say so."

"I do."

"Okay. We'll go somewhere else. Cornwall. I know people in Penzance. I'll get a job on the boats. You can make good money on the boats. And you can get some rest."

"I don't need a rest. I need a life."

"Then you can get a life."

"And where are we going to live while we're doing this? Have you thought about that?"

"We'll get a flat."

She shook her head. "You're very sure about this."

"Someone has to be."

She poured some wine into her glass and said "You're mad. Mad to come back and mad to suggest this..."

"You..." he said.

"Me? What about me? I'm old enough to be your mother."

"So what? You're not my mother. You're different."

"And so are you. Probably too different for your own good." She drank. "How did you get over here?"

"I biked it."

"And how are you planning to take me to Wales or Cornwall or wherever you think of next? I'm not going on a bike."

"We'll go in the Toyota."

She laughed again. "It's a heap of junk. We'd be lucky to get as far as Maidstone."

"We'll take the risk."

"Along with all the others."

"And what are they?"

"He'll come looking for us."

"So we'll be ready for him."

"And he'll get other people looking for us."

"Oh, now I'm scared."

"He won't give up."

"Nor will I."

Anne swirled her glass and took another mouthful of wine. "I'd offer you a drink, but you have to leave now." She turned her head towards the sound of a car. "That could be him."

"Okay."

The car passed the entrance to the drive and carried on down the road.

"But if you want…"

"Yes?"

'If you want, come back tomorrow. He'll be in Canterbury all day…"

"I'll be here. What time?"

"Midday?"

"Okay."

"Just make sure Bert doesn't see you…"

Fargo leaned in to kiss her. She smelt of lemons. She hesitated for a moment, then let him plant a quick one on her lips. "Don't worry," he said, and he cupped her face with his hands.

"That's easy for you to say."

"Easy said, easy done. Easy."

"And then?"

He shrugged. "We do what we're meant to do?"

She almost smiled but her face ached, and the skin around her mouth felt pinched with nothing.

*

That night, as Anne lay in bed and listened to Harry snoring, she imagined herself in a new life. Her mind turned heavy and swollen in her head, and voices whispered behind her eyes. "Crazy," they said, "crazy, crazy, mad, mad, crazy." She heard distant traffic and the call of dark birds. Were these signs? She didn't believe in signs. There were no such things. Signs and beliefs and superstitions were for weak people. But stop. Now her fingers were tingling, and her toes were hot.

She'd tried to imagine a new life before. She'd even saved money from the house-keeping Harry gave her, and stashed it in a bag at the back of her wardrobe. She hadn't counted it lately but there was at least nine grand there. Maybe a bit more. "Running money" she called it, though she'd never thought she'd use it for running. But now she was thinking, thinking about running with purpose and the idea that it was half possible. So the idea might have been stupid and dangerous and doomed, but it was an idea, and any idea was a good thing. She had friends, women she met for lunch in town, and when she'd confided in them about Harry, about how he smelt of pork and made clicking sounds when he snoozed in front of the television, they told her that their husbands did the same and she was lucky. Her kids had left, she could do whatever she wanted. But there was no idea behind this luck, and no promise. There was just regret.

Five years earlier, her mother had died in a nursing home. Anne had visited her every day, and a week before the old woman passed away, she'd talked about regret. "I wish," she said, "I'd lived my own life."

"Haven't you?" said Anne.

"No."

"But I thought you and Father…"

The old woman raised a finger. "I've lived the life other people expected of me. I was going to do things, things for myself, but I never did. I spent too much time working. And when I wasn't working I felt guilty that I wasn't working. What sort of life is that?"

"No," said Anne, "you don't mean that," but as she said the words and stroked the back of her mother's birdy hand, she recognised the thought. It sneaked up on her, crashed into her own lake of regret and mingled with the idea that that she'd never expressed her feelings or allowed herself to be happier.

"I mean everything I say," said her mother. "I didn't used to, but I suppose that's part of it, isn't it? Part of living your own life…" and she closed her eyes and dozed.

Live your own life. Is this the secret of life? Is this its meaning? Are these the four words – so obvious, waiting and plain – we spend our lives searching for? Are these the words priests hide from us, the ones they keep in their robes because they contradict the lies they tell? Is it this simple? Anne turned over and stared at the curtains. The shadows of trees played against them, the wind blew, leaves curled through the air. Is it this simple?

It was too difficult to be the woman she wanted to be. She was constricted by her husband, and when she thought about Fargo, she knew that however good she felt when she was with him, she would still end up feeling lost. But maybe being lost with someone who smelt of tar was worth the trouble. Or maybe not. She didn't know. She closed her eyes, watched the spots that gathered in the black, and willed herself to sleep.

In the morning, she cooked breakfast. The atmosphere in the kitchen was thick, and as Harry chewed sausage and she nibbled the corner of a piece of toast, he stared at her. She was tired but he didn't care. His face was red and his blood pressure was tipping but she didn't care. He dabbed his forehead. She waited for him to say something but he had nothing to say. He liked the silence and the knowledge that he owned her. Possession was everything to him, and when he left the house, he said "I'll have pork chops for tea…" and slammed the door before she had a chance to answer or ask if he'd like them burnt. And as she watched him walk to his car she cursed his back, picked up the dirty plates, stacked them in the dishwasher, went upstairs, sat on the bed and stared at the floor.

She stared at the floor for half an hour. The carpet was a cream colour. She'd chosen it. She remembered the day. A day filled with the future, the smell of fresh paint and the taste of sweet coffee. She looked at her toes. They were carefully painted. She checked the time. It was half past eight. She thought about Fargo. She hadn't made a decision. She had three and a half hours. She could change her life. She could put the stress on any word she wanted. She lay back, picked up a magazine and flicked through it. She found an article and started to read. It was an interview with a writer. The woman was talking to the interviewer about climate change, about how it was everyone's responsibility to think about the consequences of their actions, and how writers were the guardians of the planet's conscience. And how when she drove from her house in London to her cottage in Cornwall, she was often overwhelmed by the weight of the burden she was carrying. "We," she said, "are on the cusp. Our eyes are closed, we're walking towards a cliff, and no one knows what's around the corner." Anne closed the magazine, tossed it onto the floor and went to have a shower. As she stood in the water, her mother's words came back to her, echoing over and over and over in her head. "I wish I'd lived my own life." Then they found their way to her lips. "Live your own life, Anne." She said the words, and then she shouted them and tears came to her eyes and clarity broke through the mist.

*

Fargo packed his bag and caught a bus to Broadstairs. Maybe Anne had packed her own bag and pulled the car out of the garage and was waiting for him, or maybe she wasn't. But he didn't have anything else to do and anyway, it was a nice day. The rain had stopped and between the clouds there were patches of blue sky. The sun came out. The sun went in. The sun came out again. The west brightened.

He got out at the nearest stop, walked the mile to Hyde Hall and found a place where he could look through the hedge. He saw Bert pushing a wheelbarrow. He saw open curtains. He didn't see a car. He waited until Bert was out of sight, then walked up the drive to the front door. He rang the bell, stood back and waited.

He didn't have to wait. The door opened, Anne reached out, grabbed his jacket and pulled him inside. "Okay," she said, "if we're going to do this, we do it now. If I think about it any more, I'll change my mind."

"What?"

"What what?"

"You heard me."

"I did, but are you sure?"

"Don't ask. I might give you the wrong answer." She turned and went to the kitchen. He followed. "There," she said. "Keys to the car. Get it going and wait for me." Radar was snoozing by his bowl. He opened his eyes and stared at Fargo.

"Okay," he said, and he went out the back door, around the side of the house to the garage. The Toyota was waiting. He opened the boot and dropped his bag in. He looked around. Sitting on a bench at the bag of the garage were some cases of wine. "Nice," he said, and he grabbed one and put it next to his bag. He picked up a useful penknife. He had that. And then he got into the driver's seat, fired up the engine, sat with his hands in the wheel and waited. A minute later, Anne and Radar appeared and threw two bags onto the back seat. Radar barked, jumped in with the bags, Anne sat in the front and said "So? What are you waiting for?"

"The dog's coming too?"

"Radar hates Harry. Harry hates Radar. I don't think it would be a good idea to leave them together."

"Okay…" He rested his hands on the steering wheel and stared through the windscreen.

"You know how to drive?"

"Of course I know how to drive."

"Prove it."

"Okay."

He drove out of the garage, steered around the corner, missed Bert by six inches and stalled the car. The old man was carrying a flowerpot. He dropped the pot. It smashed on the drive, and when he saw Anne, he said "Oh hello, Mrs Swaine. Don't you worry… I'll…" but he didn't finish what he was saying to her and said to Fargo "What the hell are you doing here?"

"Bert…" Anne said.

"I was told he wasn't to come here again."

"He's just picking some things up."

"Yeah," said Fargo. "And he's got to go now," and he gunned the car, crushed the remains of the flowerpots, swung down the drive and through the gates. He stopped to let the traffic pass and watched as Bert stumbled towards them, his mouth open in a big O. Radar turned and looked at the old man and barked. Fargo turned right into the road and then they were gone.

*

They drove in silence for ten minutes, through the outskirts of the town to the Canterbury road. When they reached a place where the view opened up and the fields stretched towards Pegwell Bay, Anne turned to Fargo and said "Okay…"

"Yeah." he said.

"You've got a plan?"

"Sort of."

"You going to tell me about it?"

"Wales. We're going to Wales. Unless you've got a better idea."

"No. Sounds good to me. As long as it's far enough away from him."

"It'll be far enough."

They drove in silence for a few more minutes.

"And when we get there?"

"I'll get a job. Like I said…"

"And where will we live?"

"I've got a couple of hundred quid."

"That's going to pay for the petrol…"

"How much have you got?"

"Nine grand."

"There you go," he said.

"Yeah. There we go," she said, and as he turned onto the road towards Whitstable and the M2, she wound down the window, let the fresh air blow through her hair, reached out and touched the back of Fargo's neck. She stroked the hairs that grew there, closed her eyes and for a moment, wondered if she was mad or just crazy. But when she opened them again and saw the smile on Fargo's face and the dimple in his cheek, doubt hid its face and crawled away. Live your own life.

Ten miles away, Harry left his Whitstable shop, climbed into his car, and drove east. His thoughts were running fast and plenty. That morning, a supplier had offered him eight boxes of donkey meat – would he use it in sausages or hamburgers? Would he tell Clare, one of the assistants in his Margate shop, that she would get a box of chops in return for an accommodation in the back office? Should he tell the Sweet twins from the wholesalers that a hundred quid was theirs if they broke Fargo's legs? Should he lock Anne in her bedroom for a couple of days? And as he headed towards Broadstairs, he wondered if he should buy a new car. Maybe an SL. A convertible. Silver. And maybe he'd sell Anne's Toyota. It was embarrassing to see it parked in his drive and besides, what did she need a car for? All she needed was another slap. And as he turned this thought over in his head and watched its facets catch the brutal light of his imagination, he recognised the very car he was thinking about. Travelling west, it was approaching the roundabout he was approaching from the east. It stopped to let some traffic though, then headed towards him and passed on his right. As it did, the driver looked at him, and then the passenger. For a moment, Fargo's face froze, but then he raised a hand and smiled, and Anne stared straight ahead before they accelerated away and onto the dual carriageway.

The shock was great. He felt a twinge in his chest and for a moment he couldn't do what his head told him to do. He simply sat there and watched the traffic swirl, and felt sweat bubble on his forehead. A moment later he was bought out of his trance by the beeping horn of the car behind and when he looked in the mirror, a clenched fist. He waited for three cars to pass in front, then pulled out, squealed around the roundabout and headed back the way he'd come.

In the Toyota, Fargo was gunning it and Radar, who had been dozing on the back seat, sat up to see what the hurry was about. Anne looked over her shoulder. A mile away, Harry was stuck behind a white van driven by a man from Folkestone who was delivering a wardrobe to a woman in Sittingbourne. Another mile further down the road, tucked behind a fence by the Frost Farm slip, RPU Officer Steven Joyce was sitting in his marked Volvo, eating a salad sandwich and watching a hovering kestrel. He was a vegetarian and thinking deeply, recalling a recent holiday in Orkney where he and his wife had spent a week bird watching. They'd seen curlews, lapwings, red-throated divers, snipe, skuas, petrels, fulmars, turnstones, terns, guillemots, ravens, oyster catchers, golden plovers, redshanks and now, as he stared at the kestrel, he considered his options. He could take early retirement and buy a cottage in Lerwick with a garden and views of the tide from the upstairs windows. Then he could set up his scope and watch the birds in peace, keep a diary, maybe take a walk out to Fetlar to look for the red-necked phalarope before coming back to light a fire and toast his toes and forget about the fools he had to deal with every day. The fools who drove at 90 in a 60 limit, or 40 in a 20. Fools like this fool in a Toyota who cruised by at 75. He looked at his watch. His shift was over in an hour. He could let the car go. He would.

In the Toyota, Fargo was keeping one eye on the rear-view mirror and the other on the road. Radar made a wheezing sound and farted, and Anne said "He looked rather unhappy."

"I think he was more than unhappy."

Harry was steaming. He overtook the white van and came up behind a dawdling mini-bus. He flashed his lights and beeped hard on his horn, and as the bus pulled over, he squeezed past, floored the accelerator and smiled as the turbo kicked in and pushed the car to 80, 85, 90. A gentle bend was coming up, and as he took it, he saw the Toyota, maybe half a mile ahead. His speed hit 97 and as it did, blue lights suddenly appeared in all his mirrors, and the wail of sirens filled the air. For a moment, folly overtook reason and he thought about trying to outrun the cop, but then he slapped the palm of his hand against his forehead, indicated left and started to slow down. A minute later he was sitting on the hard shoulder and RPU Officer Steven Joyce was climbing out of his car, pulling on his patrol cap and taking out a notebook. Harry Swaine was leaning forward, his head pressed against the rim of the steering wheel. A mile away, Fargo Hawkins, who had seen everything in his rear-view mirror, slowed the Toyota to 70, looked at Anne and shook his head. "I think he's going to be well pissed off now."

"Why?"

He thumbed over his shoulder. "The cops just pulled him over."

Anne looked behind, saw the flashing blue lights and then they disappeared and she smiled and said "He's already got nine points."

"Oh dear," said Fargo.

"I know," said Anne. She touched her face and winced. "Isn't it a shame?"

*

Derek Muir was a family man. He lived in Ramsgate, in a tidy house on the east cliff. There were no ghosts in his past. He didn't have a beard, he'd never owned a canoe, he didn't have issues and he wasn't challenged. He loved his wife and his teenage kids were well behaved. He'd spent twenty-one years as a policeman, took early retirement, spent six months gardening and doing jobs around his house, but one day he woke up and realised he was bored. He missed something.

So he sat down, considered his life, took advice from an ex-colleague and within the month had joined UKTecs, a firm of Private Investigators with headquarters in London and offices throughout the country. He joined a team based in Canterbury, and was given an office in a tall building with a view of the cathedral.

The company's website outlined the services on offer – "Tracing Missing Persons, Matrimonial Surveillance, Background Checks, Pre-nup Screening…" the list was long and comprehensive, and the page that outlined his own experience stressed the fact that his work as a decorated police officer had provided him with unrivalled courage, knowledge and insight.

He settled into the work, built a solid reputation for discretion and tact, produced results and adapted his skills to the work. When clients were shown into his office, they knew they were meeting an honest man. A well ordered office, a certificate from the Alliance of Professional Private Investigators on the wall, a box of tissues on a low table, a selection of earnest books, a tidy desk, an efficient secretary called Brenda who might have been a librarian but wasn't, a decent cup of tea or coffee, and a selection of quality biscuits. But when, the morning after he'd been pulled over by the cops, Harry Swaine called in without an appointment, and said "Found you in Yellow Pages. I need you to find someone…" biscuits weren't required.

"I'm sorry?"

Brenda stood in the door with a pale face and a pad of paper. "Mr Swaine hasn't got…' she said.

Derek smiled at her and said "It's okay, Brenda. Close the door…" and to Harry, "Please come in," and he pointed to a chair.

Harry nodded, stepped into the office, sat and said "Before I say anything, can I count on you?"

"Count on me?"

"Yes. I'm talking about discretion. I could go to the police, but I don't want them involved. And I'm not having it in the papers, not anywhere near. I've got a business, a reputation to think about. This is…" and Harry leant forward "between you and me."

"Of course."

"And when I say you and me, I mean it." He thumbed towards the door. "I don't want Miss Marple sticking her oar in."

"I can assure you that Brenda is more than discrete."

"And what does that mean?"

"Mr Swaine..."

"Yes?"

"As a company, we're bound by the APPI's code of ethics, and that means we would never, under any circumstances, divulge details of our investigations to any outside agency. Unless of course..."

"Unless of course what?"

"Unless there's evidence of criminality. Then, of course, we'd be obliged to contact the police."

"Fair enough."

"Is there evidence of..."

"My wife has run off with my gardener. My ex-gardener. Unless that's a crime, the police don't need to know a thing, and nor does anyone else. All I want you to do is find them."

"Please be assured, Mr Swaine, that as soon as I receive your instructions, our discretion is guaranteed."

"And the likelihood that you'll find them?

"Well that, of course, depends. If you want us to take your instructions, I'll lead the investigation, but we have offices from Penzance to Inverness, and anything you tell us will be passed onto them, and other investigators will be briefed to look out for them. So unless they leave the country, I think a successful outcome is probably a given. And if they do manage to get abroad, we have relationships with agencies in Europe, the States and..."

"Hang on..."

"Yes?"

"One minute you're telling me that this is going to be between you and me, the next we've got every snoop between here and Scotland knowing my business." He stood up.

"Mr Swaine. I'll be the only one who knows the details. All anyone else will know is physical descriptions, registration number of the car, that sort of thing. They won't know why they're looking for them, who they are, but nothing else..."

"Good." He sat down again. "And it'll stay that way?"

"Of course."

"You can guarantee that?"

"If you decide to use our services, it'll be in the contract."

"It'd better be."

Derek made a note, adjusted his shirt cuffs and said "So when did you last see your wife? Your wife and, who was it?"

"My ex-gardener. Yesterday."

"Where?"

"On the A299. Driving a Toyota Corolla."

"Colour? Reg?"

Harry told him, Derek made a note, Harry shook his head, Derek said "More tea?" Harry shook his head.

"Do you have any idea where they were going?"

"No."

"And you're sure they weren't just out for the day?"

"Out for the day? What? Lunch in the pub and a pleasant stroll around Herne Bay?"

"I have to ask, Mr Swaine. In most cases, missing persons return home within 48 hours. Whatever you might think, whatever you might read, an actual disappearance is rare."

"Look." Harry leaned forward and put his hands on Derek's desk. "My wife's done a runner with the sack of spunk I used to employ as my gardener. As far as I'm concerned, he can go fuck himself, but I want her back."

"Of course." Derek didn't like clients touching his desk, but there was little he could do about it. It was one of his foibles. "Do you know if either of them have a mobile?"

"Of course they have, but I've already tried them. They're switched off. Either that or they're not picking up."

"Can I have the numbers, please?"

"I told you, they're not picking up…"

Derek rolled his eyes now and folded his arms. "Mr Swaine? Are you going to let me do my job?"

"Yes. But what have their phones…"

"Along with the car, they're the most important lead we've got. They might not be picking up to you, but they'll be picking up to someone else. That's a given. And making calls…"

Harry leant back, took out his phone and started to scroll. Derek looked at the fatty prints the man had left on his desk. They looked like the ghosts of sausages floating in a pond of gravy.

"Okay. Here you go," and Harry read out Anne's number, then Fargo's.

Derek wrote them down and said "If there's anything else you can think of…"

"Like what?"

"Maybe your wife had talked about a place she wanted to visit, that sort of thing."

"I don't know. She was always on about going somewhere. One day it was Devon, the next Wales…"

"Okay. When you get home, take a look through her things. Sometimes, even though people think they don't want to be found, they do. They leave clues."

"If I find anything, I'll let you know."

"Is there anything else you think I should know?"

"What do you mean?"

"For example, have you any idea why she left?"

Harry shrugged. "Who knows? Maybe she thinks twenty minutes in the sack with a twenty-year-old kid is worth more than thirty years of marriage."

"Okay."

"Oh, and they took the dog."

"They took your dog?"

"Hers. She's welcome to it. Knackered old thing. Smells like a drain."

"Good."

"Good?"

"A twenty-year-old boy, a fifty-five-year-old woman, an old dog, a Toyota Corolla. It'd be difficult to miss a party like that. So, if there's nothing else you can think of, there are a couple of formalities. That's if you want to engage our services…"

"Where do I sign?"

"It's a no find, no fee service…"

"Fair enough…"

"As long as they're still in the UK. If they travel abroad, charges will apply, but we can cross that bridge when we come to it. As I said, we have associates we can call on…" Derek opened a desk drawer, pulled out a folder and said "This is a standard form, and if you're happy with it…"

"Do I look happy?"

"Maybe you'd like to take it away and read it, then come back tomorrow to confirm your instructions?"

"No. Give me a pen. You start today. Now."

*

Sixty miles away, in Sevenoaks, Fargo and Anne spent the night in a room over a pub. They only unpacked what they needed, lay on the bed, ate a plate of sandwiches, drank a bottle of wine, shared an apple, listened to the sound of the drinkers in the bar below and then they slept.

They woke at half five and an hour later, as they lay in a heap of sheets and duvet and pillows and drank tea, and Radar snored on a blanket under the window, she rested her head on his chest, took a deep breath and said "There's something I have to know."

"Go on."

"What do I mean to you?"

Fargo sat up and scratched his head. "What do I mean to you?"

"Yes."

"What do you mean?"

"Well, I'm old enough to be, you know…" she stopped.

He nodded. "It's okay…"

"Thank you." She reached up and touched his chin. "And most lads your age are going out with girls their age."

"Have you met any girls my age?"

"One or two."

"Okay. So I've been out with a few, and after a couple of weeks it just gets boring."

"And it's not going to get boring with me?"

He shook his head. "You're different. You know stuff. You're interested in stuff. And you…"

"Me?"

"Yes…" He thought, trying to get the words right. "You… you don't care."

Anne laughed. "And what does that mean?"

"I don't think you care what people think. You want to go your own way…"

"That's true."

"And most people, they're only interested in what people think about them. They want other people to envy them, you know, the car they drive, the clothes they wear, the holidays they take. You don't give a toss."

"I like a good bottle of wine. I like going to art galleries. I love reading. When I get the chance, I like to visit new places."

"Yeah, but I don't think you want everyone to know."

"I don't…"

"So there you go. You don't boast about it. That's what you mean to me."

"And the rest?"

"The rest? What's that?"

"What we spent the last hour doing."

"It's amazing."

Anne laughed again. "You don't have to be nice, Fargo. You can just tell the truth. I can take it."

"Okay. Here's the truth. Every other girl I've slept with has spent most of the time worrying about whether her makeup will get smudged. You… you just go for it. And you know what you're doing."

"So do you."

"I've had a bit of practice…"

"I bet you have."

"But never with someone like you."

Anne laughed, lifted her head towards him and kissed him. Radar sat up at the sound and farted. The evening before, they'd bought him two bowls, a sack of beef 'n' rice complete dog food, and a selection of knotted rawhide chews.

"You want?"

"No," she said. "We've got to get moving."

"Aw..."

"Really."

"Really?"

"Really."

"Shame."

"Shower and then off, Fargo."

"Okay."

*

The sky was full and grey, the roads ran with rain, the car windows misted, birds huddled under eaves and drains backed up, but as Anne, Fargo and Radar left the A21 and joined the M25 at junction 5, they felt protected by the weather.

They'd made decisions. They were going to Wales. Once they were away from the M25, they were going to avoid motorways. If they had to spend the night anywhere, they'd stay in B&Bs or hotels with car parks round the back. If the B&Bs wouldn't allow Radar in the room, they'd either (a) smuggle him in using a sack or (b) make him comfortable in the car.

"We'd need a huge sack," said Fargo.

Anne thought about saying something obvious, but didn't. "People love Radar."

"Of course they do."

"They can't resist him. I mean, the people in that pub – they didn't bat an eyelid."

"True."

Other decisions had been made. She was going to phone her sons, he was going to get a job in a Welsh pub, and the next time they bought food for Radar they'd ask for a brand that was less likely to induce flatulence.

"Remember the first time I suggested you leave?"

"Yes…"

"You said you hadn't made a decision for years."

"So?"

"You've just made half a dozen."

She leaned towards him and kissed his neck and said "Have you any idea how good I feel?"

"If it's as good as I'm feeling…"

"And how good are you feeling?"

"Better than good, Anne… Free."

She nodded, and then said "Do something for me."

"Sure."

"Stop calling me Anne. Call me Miss Carter."

"Miss Carter? Why Miss Carter?"

"It was my maiden name. And I've never liked Anne. Makes me think I should have green gables."

"What?"

"Pardon me, Miss Carter…"

"What?"

"Oh never mind, Fargo." She reached over and squeezed his thigh. "Just drive the car."

*

Harry spent the morning at Hyde Hall. He started in the kitchen, rifling through drawers and cupboards, pulling out cards and notebooks and envelopes and tickets from dry cleaners. Everything smelt of Anne and everything irritated him – the way she kept plastic bags rolled up, the neat rows of cleaning products, tall ones on the left, stubby ones on the right, and the way all the mugs and cups and glasses were arranged in perfect little groups. He found a black plastic bag and began stuffing it with shopping lists and half-used cleaning cloths and washing-up sponges – when it was full he dragged it to the back door, tossed it outside and grabbed another. He opened a drawer and nicked the end of his finger on the handle. Blood came, and as it dripped onto the floor, a familiar switch flipped in his head. He dropped the bag, kicked it across the floor, grabbed a broom, weighed it in his hands, allowed himself a small smile then smashed it into a plate rack. The noise of the crockery smashing filled him with pleasure, so he turned to a glass-fronted cupboard, took a step back and took a swing. The leaded panes shattered and a collection of bowls, egg cups and dishes exploded. Next, a shelf of crystal glasses, tumblers and flutes. Gone. Two drawers of knives and forks, pulled out and thrown across the breakfast bar. A toaster lobbed at the French windows, a kick to the door of the fridge, another to the door of the oven, a hammer found and used on Portuguese tiles. And then, food and drink.

A box of cornflakes, ripped open and tossed in an arc, a bottle of milk flung towards the ceiling, sugar, coffee, tea bags, apples and oranges. A bottle of wine cart-wheeling, another bottle of wine, a third. All accompanied by roars and shouts and screams, so by the time a fourth bottle of wine was winging its way towards a picture of horses on a beach, Bert was standing by the French windows, staring in and wondering whether to knock on the glass. When Harry saw him, he yelled "What the fuck are you looking at?"

Bert shook his head, turned and headed back towards the garden.

"No! Bert!"

Bert didn't hear.

Harry ran to the windows, opened them and yelled "Bert!" again.

Bert turned. "Sir?"

The two men faced each other. There were gulfs between them – wealth, ambition, rage, hatred, possession and age – but the truth was simple. They'd both been born in the back room of houses in a poor area of Ramsgate, they'd both been sent to school with holes in their shoes. "Just letting off a bit of steam," said Harry.

Bert didn't know what to say.

"Mrs Swaine's gone off with that... that..." he couldn't say Fargo's name.

"She's really gone?"

"Yes."

"I saw them driving away the other day, but I thought... well, I don't know what I thought."

"You saw them?"

"Yes, sir. I tried to stop them, but they almost ran me over."

"Bastards."

Bert looked towards the kitchen. "Is there anything I can do?"

"No. Get back to the garden. I'll sort the kitchen," and he went back indoors to start on Anne's clothes.

*

Derek Muir had met a few clients like Harry Swaine, people who told half the truth, egos who saw humiliation hanging from every lamp post, fat men who smelt of meat, bullies who hit their wives and then wondered why they'd done a runner. And most dangerous of all, control freaks who'd lost control. But a contract had been signed so he tidied his notes, wrote them up and emailed all UKTecs' offices, with a particular memo for colleagues in Bristol, Exeter, Plymouth, Cardiff, Aberystwyth, Shrewsbury, Bangor and Liverpool. "Client tells me targets might be heading for Devon or Wales. Maybe. No idea where, but as you can see from spec. notes, we've got plenty to go on. My hunch is the wife will get tired of the boy and she'll go home with her tail between the proverbial. That's if the boy doesn't realise there's no money in it first. So I reckon the case will be closed by the end of the week, but keep your eyes peeled anyway. Bests." Then he looked outside and checked the weather. Rain was falling in ripe, swirling columns, pooling in the gutters and pouring off roofs. He went for lunch.

He dripped in the corner of a pub, ate a cheese sandwich, drank a pint of soda and lime and read the local paper. He liked the local paper. It was packed with grief and fun. He read a story about a woman who had been evicted from her local authority maisonette for keeping eight snakes in the bathroom, and another about a wedding that had descended into chaos when the groom had been discovered in flagrante with his new mother-in-law in a hotel toilet. Two donkeys had been stolen from a field outside Sandwich and their owners were "frantic with worry", while in Ramsgate, two pairs of clippers had been stolen from a dog grooming parlour. He was halfway through a story about the dangers of abandoned fridges when his phone rang.

"Hello darling." It was his wife, Rachel. "Everything okay?"

"We've got a leak in the bedroom," she said. "I've had to put a bucket down to catch the drips. I went out to have a look, and I think a tile's slipped."

"I'll call Ian." Ian was a neighbour, a builder.

"Already done," she said. "He's on his way."

"Okay. Let me know how he gets on."

"Sure. Oh, and don't forget to pick up the dry cleaning on your way home."

"It's on my list."

"What time will we be leaving?"

"The usual."

"Okay then."

Derek heard the sound of the front door bell.

"That'll be Ian," said Rachel.

"Speak later."

"Bye."

Derek finished his sandwich and thought about his wife, his children and how if a slipped tile was his family's version of a crisis, then he was a lucky man. He folded the newspaper, stood up and went to the bar. "Thanks, George," he said to the barman. "Cheers, Derek," said George, and as he stepped out into the rain, he wondered at the poetry of the mundane, and how God was good and watched over his world with a fly's eyes.

*

Fargo left the motorway and headed towards Guildford. The traffic was steady and behaved, lights on, rolling west, hissing with spray. Anne snoozed for a while and woke up as they were negotiating a roundabout outside Aldershot. She rubbed her eyes, yawned, stared at the road for a few minutes and then said "Weird…"

"What's weird?"

"I had a dream."

"Going to tell me about it?"

She squinted at the rain. "I was walking. Yes. I was walking along a path, and there were enormous trees and bushes, and parrots were flying and screeching. The sun was bright. Hot. There was a wide river, and steam. I think it was the Amazon jungle or somewhere like that, and as I walked further into it, I knew I was going to get lost."

"And did you?"

"Yes. The path got narrow and climbed a hill, and when I knew I was in trouble, I turned around and walked back the way I'd come. Then I found a door in a wall and opened it, and I was standing in a sort of courtyard, like one of those you get in an old university. It was calm and quiet, and when I looked around I saw my boys sitting on a bench."

"Your boys?"

"My sons. They were smiling at me and I waved at them, and when I looked up at my hand it caught fire. It didn't feel hot though, it felt normal. And then I woke up." She stared out of the window. Fargo looked at the side of her face. A curl of hair dropped down over her eyes. She flicked it away and shook her head. He said "Know what I think?"

"About what?"

"About dreams."

"Tell me."

"I reckon dreams are your mind taking a shit."

She laughed and said "That's funny." She reached over and took his arm and squeezed it. She loved the feel of his arm. He was strong and so soft. "And stupid."

"Thanks."

"My pleasure."

They drove on for another couple of miles, and then she said "I've got to call Mike."

"Mike?"

"My eldest. Can we stop soon?"

"Whenever you like. We'll get some coffee."

Twenty minutes later, they were parked behind a pub, Fargo was inside ordering and Anne was on her phone, walking in a wide circle, an umbrella up, dodging the puddles, talking.

Mike was her sensitive and thoughtful one. He lived in Brighton and worked as a social worker. She asked him if he'd spoken to his father, and when he said he hadn't spoken to him for a couple of months, she said "I've left him."

He didn't miss a beat. "About bloody time," he said. "What happened?"

"You want the gory details?"

"Mum, at the moment I'm dealing with a case that would give you nightmares, so nothing you say is going to shock me."

"He hit me for the last time."

There was a silence on the line, then "Did you call the police?"

Anne laughed. "That would only have made things worse. Besides, what would they have done?"

"They could do a lot."

"No. I did what I've been meaning to do for years."

"So where are you? What are you doing?"

"I'm in a pub car park… somewhere near Guildford."

"What?"

"It's not as bad as it sounds."

"Are you safe?"

"Of course."

"Are you with any one?"

Silence.

"Mum? Are you with any one?"

"Yes."

"Who?"

"Fargo."

"What's Fargo?"

"He was a gardener. Used to work at the Hall."

"You're kidding me."

"No."

"The gardener? He's my age, Mum."

"Michael. Are you judging me?"

"No, but…"

"But nothing, Mike. Did I ever judge you? And when your father threw you out, who stood by you? Who defended you?"

"Okay, Mum. We've gone through that, and I'm not going through it again. But please..."

"But please what? Men can go off with women half their age, men can go off with men half their age. And you know all about that, don't you?"

"So?"

"But as soon as a woman does it..."

"Point taken. But..."

"But what?"

"Well, are you... er... are you..."

"Sleeping with him?"

"Yes."

"Yes, Mike. And if you want to know, it's amazing. And besides that, he makes me happy. He's kind and gentle and funny. He talks. He listens. He's polite. He's everything your father isn't. Wasn't."

"Okay. But.."

"But nothing, Mike. Nothing."

"Mum..."

"Hang on..." The rain had got heavier, so she took shelter in the pub porch, sat on a little bench and stared at a poster that extolled the benefits of eating more fruit. "Are you cross with me?"

"Of course not. Maybe worried, but not cross. If you want to know, I suppose I think you're very brave. Have you got money?"

"Yes."

"And your car?"

"Yes."

"So where are you going?"

"If I tell you, you'll keep quiet about it? You won't say anything to your father, not for now, anyway."

"My lips are sealed."

"Okay. We're not sure. Wales, I think."

"Wales?"

"Yes. Fargo thinks he knows somewhere he can get work."

"And what are you going to do?"

"I'm going to be who I was going to be years ago."

"Before we got in the way?"

"You never got in the way."

"Not even Robert?"

"No. Not even Robert."

"Have you spoken to him?"

"Not yet."

"You going to?"

"Of course. But you know Robert. I'll need to choose the right moment."

"Is there ever a right moment with Robert?"

"Good question."

*

Harry made a good job of Anne's clothes. He started with her dresses, skirts and trousers, slicing them with a butcher's knife, then re-hanging them so they looked neat and untouched. He cut holes in the backs of her blouses and sweaters and then moved onto her drawers of lingerie, shredding everything he could find. Soon the floor was covered in a blizzard of cotton, satin, silk, lycra and lace. He carefully scooped the pieces up and placed them back in the drawers, then fetched a can of aerosol paint from the garage, arranged her shoes on newspaper, and sprayed them inside and out. He did the same with a collection of hats and then, as his pièce de résistance, sprayed "SLAG" on the back of her coats, and while he let the paint dry, went downstairs and had a whisky.

As he sat and let the drink do its thing, he allowed himself a smile, and this turned into a laugh, which, after a few minutes, turned into hysteria. He snorted and howled, kicked a table, calmed down, poured another glass of whisky, looked at his watch, realised he was hungry, grabbed his phone, called an Indian takeaway, said "Just bring me something hot. Plenty of meat. Lamb. Enough for two..." hung up and waited.

As he waited, he watched television and thought this was the way he was meant to live his life. So he didn't have a woman to cook his meals and wash his shirts and clean the floors, but he could buy one. And maybe he'd have a few people round, people who liked a drink and a laugh, and he'd let them put their feet on the tables and put glasses down without using coasters. He didn't like music but he'd blast some anyway, and if people wanted to smoke, they could smoke. And if they wanted to strip off and jump naked into the swimming pool, they could. In fact, he'd encourage it. It'd be on the invitation. And the more he thought about it, the better the idea felt. So he grabbed a pen and wrote "Two fingers to the rain! Open House at Hyde Hall! Bacon butties! Sausage rolls! Hog roast! Cold beer! Warm beer! Indoor smoking! Compulsory skinny dipping!" And then he started to make a list of people to invite. He started with the managers of his shops, and added some of the assistants and a couple of wholesalers. Then he moved on to chefs and waiting staff from the hotels and restaurants he supplied, and a couple of hacks from local newspapers, and by the time he'd reached the bottom of the page he had thirty-five names. So he couldn't count a single one of them as a friend, but he didn't care. Friendship was overrated and rooted in weakness. He didn't want people depending on him and he wasn't going to depend on anyone. And before anyone said "Yeah, but what about Anne?" dependency had nothing to do with that relationship. She belonged to him, she was a possession. So she'd kicked his ego but she was nothing without him, and when he got her back she'd know it.

*

Twenty miles away, Derek Muir ate his dinner. Sally, his daughter, sat on one side of the table, Alfred, his son on the other, and his wife Rachel sat opposite. They were eating cold quiche, a potato salad and green beans in a light vinaigrette. He'd made the quiche, she'd made the salads, and everything was served with wooden spoons from matching bowls onto plain white plates. If anyone was still hungry when they'd finished they could help themselves to tiramisu. This had been in the fridge but was now settling at room temperature.

They ate dinner together, always in the dining room, never with the television or radio on. Derek had read somewhere that families who sat down together at least once a day were successful families, and because they talked and discussed and faced each other, they didn't suffer the problems TV dinner families suffered from. Eat from a warm plate, hold your knife and fork properly, use a napkin, ask politely for the salt and pepper, say 'thank you' when you'd finished, ask if you can get down – do all these things and you won't end up with (a) teenage pregnancies (b) substance abuse or (c) loud music at an unreasonable hour. So have a conversation, but within reason. For example, Derek never discussed work at the table. It was bad enough having to deal with Kent's bin juice at the office; the last thing he was going to do was bring it home and allow it to infect his family. So once he'd established that Ian had fixed the roof and was popping round the following day to make good the plasterwork in the bedroom, he listened as his daughter told him that in two weeks, her school was visiting the museums of London, and could she have £150 to pay for the trip?

"£150?"

"Yes. We're going to the V&A in the morning and the Science Museum in the afternoon, then spend the night in a hostel. Then we go to the British Museum the next day, and somewhere else. The Maritime Museum, I think. We have to go on a boat."

"That sounds like a great trip."

"So I can go?"

"Of course."

"I want to go," said Alfred.

"Year 12s only," said Sally, smiling. "You'll have to wait."

"That's so unfair."

"Life's unfair," said Derek, "but you'll get your chance in a couple of years."

"But she gets to have all the fun."

"No I don't. Dad took you fishing last week."

"You hate fishing."

"That's not the point. You had fun."

"So?"

"You said you never had fun."

"No, I said you have all the fun. That's different."

"No it's not."

"Yes it is."

"Kids! Please! Can we have one meal which doesn't end in an argument about nothing."

"We're not arguing," said Alfred.

"No, we're not," said Sally. "We're discussing."

"Okay. Can we have one meal that doesn't involve a discussion?"

"But you're always telling us that discussion is important."

"Yeah."

"And that without discussion, things fester."

"Uncle Fester."

"Exactly."

Derek finished his dinner, folded his arms, looked at his children and smiled at Rachel. She glowed, the glow of a beautiful wife and a thoughtful, nurturing mother. He waited, but didn't have to wait long.

"What's funny?" said Sally.

"Nothing."

"Then why are you smiling?"

"Because I love you."

"Yeah, right."

"Sorry. It was £150 you wanted for your trip?"

"Dad…"

"Yes, sweetheart?"

"Nothing."

*

Fargo and Anne stayed in Salisbury. They were going to stop at a B&B in an anonymous town or a sleepy village, but Anne wanted to see the city and look at the cathedral. So they drove on and found an old hotel on a busy street. The building had a bovine theme. There were huge posters of cows on the walls, and the chairs, bar stools and sofas were covered in black and white hide. The menu was dominated by steaks, burgers and puns, and they were happy to let Radar in "As long…" the barmaid said, "as he doesn't steal a sausage."

"Does he look like he's going to steal a sausage?"

"Yes."

"He won't."

"You sure about that?"

"He's cool."

"Okay. But if he does…"

"He won't."

"Are you sure about that?"

"Does the Queen eat garlic?

"I don't know. Does she?"

"No."

"How do you know?"

"I read it. She hates it. Won't have it on the menu, even if she's entertaining French people."

Their room was on the top floor and had low, angled ceilings, and a view of medieval houses, roofs, chimneys and the cathedral. Anne leant on the sill and as she watched, floodlights came on and illuminated the spire. A bell rang, chiming the hour. The lights shone through the rain and turned it orange and soft, and Fargo came and stood next to her, and put an arm around her waist. He squeezed and she reached up and stroked the nape of his neck.

"It's so beautiful," she said.

"And so are you," he said.

"Stop it."

"No."

She smiled and said "You know, it's odd."

"What's odd?"

"I've got this anxious feeling, like something's going to happen, but at the same time I'm not worried."

"But that's a good thing."

"Odd though." She stepped away from the window and kissed his lips. He tasted of salt. "Let's go for a walk before dinner."

"Drink first?"

"Why not?"

They went downstairs and found a table in a quiet corner of the bar. She drank something dry and white, he had a pint, they squinted at some photographs of Argentinean steers and they toasted their second day. "To us," she said.

"Us."

"Still okay?"

"Of course."

"Sure?"

He looked at her, the lovely colour of her skin, the glimpse of lace through the buttons of her blouse, the way she sucked the salt off a peanut before crunching it, the wafts of perfume and the tilt of her head towards him when she was waiting for an answer to a question. "More than okay," he said. "You?"

"Sometimes I think I'm in a movie, the rest of the time I think I'm dreaming. I should be at home, stacking plates in the dish washer, listening to a fat man snore…"

"Should you?"

"Well, yes. But then I shouldn't. Obviously. I should be here. With you." She raised her glass. "Drinking wine."

"I sort of like wine," he said.

"You sort of like wine?"

"Yeah. Trouble is, I always feel stupid when I drink it."

"Stupid?"

"Yes."

"Why's that?"

"Blokes are meant to drink beer."

"Are they?"

"Well yeah. I suppose. You know, a big glass in your hand, not some namby-pamby thing like a girl would have."

Anne laughed and said "Here…" and offered him her glass. "I'm going to educate you."

"Are you?"

"Yes."

"How?"

"Taste."

"Do I have to?"

"Yes."

He tasted and squinted.

"That bad?"

"No," he said. "Maybe I could get used to it."

"The thing is, it's a slow drink. You don't neck it, you take your time. You smell it, you sip it, you let it work on you. And it's great with food. It makes a meal…"

"Lager's great with food. Gammon, pineapple and a pint. Dash of brown sauce. You can't beat it."

Anne took her glass back and smiled, and at that moment, a spark burst in her head. "Gammon and pineapple?"

"Oh yeah," he said. "My Mum used to cook it. Sunday treat. Which makes me think…"

"Makes you think what?"

"I should call Wells."

"Wells?"

"My sister."

"Of course."

"If I don't call her at least once a month, she worries…"

*

"Wells?"

"Fargo?"

"Hi."

"I was thinking about you today! How's it going?"

"Good. I'm in Salisbury."

"Salisbury? What you doing there?"

"Passing through. I packed my job in."

"But you'd only been there a few weeks. What happened?"

"Oh, you know, this and that. I'll tell you when I see you."

"Are you coming?"

"Well…" Fargo thought about it. "I could…"

"Could?"

"The thing is, I'm on my way to Wales."

"Wales?"

"Yeah."

She heard something in his voice, the catch of hesitation, fingers scratching an ache. "You okay, bro?"

"Yeah. I'm good. It's just been a bit mad. How's Ian?" Ian was her bloke.

"He's good. Out with his mates. What's been a bit mad?"

"I can't tell you on the phone."

"Are you in trouble?"

"No. Nothing like that. Well, not much."

"Now you're worrying me…"

"It's fine. Really. I'll let you know when we get back on the road."

"We?"

"Yes."

"What's her name?"

"What makes you think she's a woman?"

"Oh please, Fargo. I'm not a fool."

"Anne."

"Is she pretty?"

Now Fargo laughed and said "That's for me to know."

"Is she there? Put her on. I want to say hello…"

"She's upstairs."

"I bet she is…"

"Wells!"

"Okay. Let me know what you decide."

"Done."

*

They borrowed an umbrella from reception and took a stroll around the cathedral close. Fargo asked Anne to tell her about the big church so she told him what she knew, which wasn't a lot, but it was enough. She knew it was built on a marsh in the English Gothic style, and John Constable had painted it, and William Golding had written about it, and there was a copy of Magna Carta in the chapter house, and if you booked in advance you could climb halfway up the spire and have a wander around the balconies.

"See, there you go again," said Fargo. "Knowing stuff. And it might be boring stuff, like, you know, I'm not really interested in churches, but you make it interesting."

"Once I've got you drinking wine, I'm going to make it my business to make you love cathedrals. And I bet you went on a school trip to Canterbury."

"Yeah, but we just mucked about."

"Of course you did."

"I wish I hadn't."

"It's never too late to learn, Fargo."

"Maybe I should go back to college."

"Maybe we should both go back to college."

"That's going to happen…"

"It could."

"Yeah, right…"

"If it did, what would you study?"

"I don't know. Maybe something medical. When I was a kid I wanted to be a doctor…"

"I think you'd need to go to university to study medicine."

"Okay. I'll go to university. What about you?"

"Art history."

"What's that?"

"The history of art."

"Okay."

"But it's not just painting, it's sculpture, architecture, ceramics…"

"What's ceramics?"

"Pottery."

"Okay. I like pottery."

They walked around the side of the cathedral, the rain twitched and the sound of singing floated from an open door. They headed towards the music, stepped inside and stood for a moment. The choir was halfway through evensong and a few people were sitting in the nave, staring up at the vaults, their eyes closed, listening. Fargo felt a vague sense of embarrassment, like he'd been given flowers. He couldn't remember the last time he'd been in a church. Anne reached out and took his hand and led him to the seats, and they sat down.

An organ accompanied the singing, and as the music rose into the roof, Fargo followed it, watching as it found cracks and spaces in the old stones. Here and there a note brushed against a pane of stained glass or twinkled against a monument, and echoed back. The water in a sad font reflected the emptiness that clung to the building's tit. The sense of embarrassment deepened – what was he supposed to do? Sit and listen? Sit and say something? Stare at the floor or the ceiling or the back of his hands? He looked at Anne. He wanted advice, a clue, help. She was sitting with her head tipped back, her eyes closed, a light smile on her lips. She could have been sun bathing. He looked at the way her skin curved from her neck to her chin, and noticed the float of hairs that grew there. Her lips moved and then the music stopped and the sound of rustling filled the building.

The choir sat down, and a priest stood up and read from the Bible. He read about how Jesus spent some time with publicans and sinners, and when the Pharisees and scribes saw this, they shook their heads and murmured. But Jesus had a go at them, telling them that there would be joy in the presence of the angels over one sinner that repenteth, and here ended the lesson, and the priest bowed his head, wandered back to his place, and the choir stood up again.

They rustled and sang another tune, and this time Fargo followed Anne's lead and tipped his head, closed his eyes and let the music swirl round him. For a couple of minutes all he heard were notes and rests and the wheeze of the organ, but then, slowly, something coalesced and met the faint smell of incense that hung in the air. The palms of his hands tingled, and he felt a creeping beneath his skin, like ants were in there. They moved slowly, and when the choir hit a high note, they twitched and spun. He opened his eyes, looked at Anne and reached out for her arm. As he touched her, she opened her eyes and smiled, leant towards him and whispered "Isn't it beautiful?"

"I'm feeling a bit weird."

"Want to leave?"

He nodded.

They waited for the choir to finish, then crept away, waited by the door for a moment and stepped outside. They strolled in silence for a few minutes and Anne said "Feeling okay now?"

"Yeah. I don't know, I got hot. I thought I was going to faint."

"Maybe Jesus wants you for a sunbeam."

"What?"

"You know. The song?"

Fargo shook his head. "No," he said, "I don't think Jesus wants me for anything."

*

Bert stood under a dripping beech tree. The evening was gloomy and he felt gloomy. He watched Hyde Hall as a voyeur would, squinting in at the window as Harry staggered from kitchen to living room, bumping into doors and shelves, steadying himself against a wall, a takeaway box in one hand and a bottle of whisky in the other. He saw the dropped curry and the spilt drink, and saw a television screen reflected in the glass doors of a drinks cabinet. It was booming pop music and applause, and a hectoring man and hysterical laughter and more applause. Bert watched for five minutes, and his thoughts turned and buckled. "If I was twenty years younger…" he thought, but that's as far as the thoughts went. Except that they didn't. They repeated themselves over and over again, rattled around in his head, and he imagined himself getting in an van and chasing after Fargo and Anne and dragging them back to Hyde Hall and kicking them in the front door so they sprawled on the floor and held their jaws and begged for mercy. Because they had it coming and Mr Swaine, good Mr Swaine, Mr Swaine who had kept him on when he bought the house and told him that as long as there was a garden he was the gardener, Mr Swaine who was as good a boss as you could have in Kent, Mr Swaine who deserved a better woman than that, Mr Swaine who was honest and good, now driven to the edge by people who only thought of themselves, selfish, spiteful and malicious people... And as Bert's mind ran with these thoughts, a telephone rang.

He watched as Harry stumbled and fell, picked himself up and grabbed a phone. "Yeah?" he said.

Someone said something.

"Robert?"

"Hello Dad."

"Robert?"

"Yeah."

*

Robert, a finance analyst with a global energy company, called his father from his flat on the top floor of a converted warehouse on Bermondsey Wall. He stood on the balcony and watched the river. The water sparkled with lights and a party boat drifted by, its decks and saloons alive with music and laughter and fun. A siren wailed and the last plane of the night turned and headed for Heathrow. Downstairs, a woman laughed, and her friend started to cook a stir-fry.

"Dad?"

"Robert..."

"What the hell's going on? I spoke to Mike – he said Mum's left."

"You spoke... you spoke to Mike? You called Mike?"

"No. He called me. I wouldn't call him. You know that. But we talked."

"Wha... wha did he say?"

"Something about Mum going off with the gardener. I told him to fuck off, but he said it's true. Is it?"

"Yeash..."

"The gardener? That fucking kid?"

"I'm going… I'm going to kill 'em both… They're going to regret… regret they ever… I think…"

"Take it easy, Dad. You don't want to go that far."

"Don't you tell me to take it easy. Don't tell me…"

"Are you drunk?"

"Na. Na…"

"Hurt the boy, but leave Mum in one piece. Don't do anything you'll regret…"

"Regret?"

"Yes Dad."

"She'll regret. I'm going to rip her face off."

"No Dad. That would be a bad idea. A very bad idea."

"Ah na…" said Harry, and he fell over.

Robert didn't need this. Work was a nightmare, his personal life was imploding, and he had spent the last week with tinnitus and blurred vision. He'd made an appointment to see a doctor but had cancelled when work told him he had to fly to Frankfurt where the food had been poor, the hotel room too small and the tumbling price of oil (down from a record high in late February) had given him more grief than a dog. Now he was back and he thought he might be more than sick. Something was grumbling in his head, and if he sat still for a moment he could hear what sounded like wasps. They were everywhere and they were angry. "Dad?" he said.

"Ya?" Harry was lying on the floor.

"I've got friends. If you want, I can have a word."

"Friends?"

"Yeah. Well, not really friends. But they're useful, and if I asked them I think they could find Mum and you know…"

"Na. Sorted." Harry tried to get up. "I got someone working on it."

"Who?"

"Private inveligator... He'll find them..."

"What's his name?"

"Dunno."

Robert gave up. He didn't want to but he was tired and he'd been down this road with his father before. It wasn't an easy one to travel. "Look Dad," he said. "Get some sleep. I'll call again tomorrow."

"Yeah, good idea. You do that," he said, and he stopped trying to get up, dropped the phone and let his head rest.

*

A man in jeans and a check shirt stood at the dining room bar of the Salisbury cow hotel, chatted to the barmaid, drank a pint and checked his phone. Tall and wiry, and with an insouciant, self-contained air, he laughed and smiled, and thought about ordering a bowl of chips, but didn't. He'd get something to eat when he got home, maybe a pizza.

Twenty-five feet away, Anne ate a salmon fillet, Fargo tucked into a steak, and they shared a good bottle of Pinot Noir. When Fargo said he thought you had to drink white wine with fish, Anne said "That's one of those British things. There are no rules with wine. Apart from enjoy." She raised her glass, he raised his and they chinked.

The room was busy, and the chatter of happy diners mixed with smells from the kitchen and some poor music. "So tell me, 'cos I don't understand," said Fargo, "what was that about?"

"What was what about?"

"The singing. The prayers. The priest."

"I don't think I'm the right person to ask."

"But the thing is, those people, they're educated. They're not stupid. They know stuff. But they fall for all that."

"They fall for it because it's an easy option. Or they can't do anything else. But most of all because they're scared. They're scared of chaos, so they need something to give it order. They're scared of death, but they need to have something to look forward to. And they're scared of their mistakes, so they have to have people to tell them everything's okay. They want order, certainty and shopping lists."

"I know, but I still don't get it."

"When you can't handle the truth you make friends with hypocrisy. And when you've got faith, it's simple."

"What does that mean?"

"I heard this story on the radio. I think it was on the radio. Maybe I read it… Anyway, this bishop is at a posh dinner somewhere. The Queen's there and the Prime Minister, and the bishop gets to sit next to a diplomat from some country in the Pacific Ocean. They get talking about religion, and the man from the Pacific says that he believes a giant bird gave birth to the earth which is carried around the universe in the belly of a giant fish. And the bishop starts laughing and tells the man that he's amazed intelligent, educated people still believe stories like that. The diplomat says "but you believe the first woman was created from a man's rib, and a talking snake convinced the same woman to disobey God…" "Well, I don't believe it literally," says the Bishop. "But I thought the Bible was the word of God," says the diplomat. "It is," says the Bishop. "But sometimes God speaks in mysterious ways."

Anne spread her arms. "That's what believers say when they can't give you a straight answer. 'It's a mystery.' But there are no mysteries. This is the truth. And the truth is easy. Look at it."

"This?"

"You, me, a good bottle of wine, that man standing by the bar. Unusual décor, cars in the road. People laughing, that bloody awful music. Radar upstairs, having a snooze. You can complicate it if you want, make stuff up, but you'll only end up chasing your own tail." She pointed her fork at Fargo's plate. "How's your steak?"

"Good."

The man standing at the bar finished his pint and checked his phone again. He'd managed to get at least three good shots of Anne and Fargo, and now, as he dialled Derek Muir and listened to the dial tone, he left the bar for a moment and stepped into the street.

"Derek Muir."

"Hi Derek. Tony Nunn, Salisbury office. I left a message."

"You did. You saw a car we've been looking for?"

"Better than that, Derek. I lucked out big time. I've got them."

"Proof?"

"I'm standing outside the hotel where Mrs Anne Swaine and a Fargo Hawkins have booked a room for the night. I've seen the register. Either they're stupid or they don't care. They checked in under her name. And I've got some shots – I'll send them over."

"Good man."

"So where are you?"

"Canterbury, Kent."

"Want me to stick around?"

"Your call. Do they look set?"

"Yeah. Eating their dinner, drinking a bottle of wine. They're not going anywhere tonight. Well, maybe a stroll, but I think it's straight up to bed for those two. They've got that look in their eyes."

"Okay. I'll call the client, give him the good news, wait on his instructions. You keep an eye on the motor. Can you do that?"

"No problem. Want me to put a tracker on it?"

"Could do. But if you think we've got them, no point pushing the boat out."

"Agreed. I'll stick around until they've gone to bed, back here first thing.'

"Excellent. Once the client knows the score, I think he'll be keen to come down himself, but I'll let you know."

"You got it," said Tony Nunn, and he hung up, went back to the bar, ordered another pint and resumed his conversation with the barmaid.

*

Derek called Harry Swaine at 21:00, 21:15 and 21:25 but each time he was put through to voice mail. At 21:45 he called for the last time and left a message.

"Hello Mr Swaine, Derek Muir from UKTecs. We've got some good news – your wife has been spotted in Salisbury, Wiltshire. I've got a man watching her and the car, and he's going to call me in the morning. Success I think. Speak tomorrow."

Satisfied with his day and anxious not to spend any more of his home time thinking about work, he sat at the kitchen table and wrote a cheque for £150, and took it upstairs. He knocked on Sally's door and waited. "Yes Dad?"

"Can I come in?"

"Sure."

She was sitting on her bed, a laptop on her knees, doing whatever she did. He took a deep breath and smiled. He loved the smell of her room, the scent of vanilla and fresh clothes, and pear drops. He waved the cheque and said "There you go, sweetheart. £150. I've made it out to the school." He took out his wallet and took out a ten pound note. "And here's some spending money. Don't blow it all at once."

"Thanks Dad."

"When's the trip?"

"In a couple of weeks."

"You'll have fun."

"It's going to be great."

He put the cheque and the note on her bed and waited for a moment, just looking around. He took a step towards her dressing table and looked at the jumble of bottles and brushes, and he reached out and touched the head of the teddy bear that sat on the top of her mirror. "Flat Brian," he said. "I remember the day we gave him to you."

"You always say that."

"I know. But it seems like yesterday."

"And you always say that."

Derek nodded. "It's what Dads do."

"Yeah."

He turned and said "Okay." He wanted to say something else, something about the wonder of the cusp she was riding, that pool between being a child and being a woman, but he knew that whatever he said would sound sad, and anyway he didn't really know anything about it. All he knew was that wonders were unfurling in that room, and he needed a beer.

So he said "Goodnight" and went downstairs and took a bottle from the fridge, flipped its top and poured it into a glass. Then he went to the front room, flicked on the television news and sat down with a sigh.

Rachel was reading a book. She said "You all right, dear?"

He nodded. "Yes." He stared at a reporter who was standing in a street talking about obesity. "I'm fine." He sipped his beer. "Though sometimes I do wonder."

"What do you wonder?"

"Well, I don't know. Where to start?" He pointed at the television. "I mean, do fat people know they're fat? Are we being poisoned by complaint? Is envy the engine of the world? Are voyeurs the new angels?"

"What are you talking about, Derek?"

He shrugged. "I'm not sure," he said, and he closed his eyes, watched the spots that gathered there and let the day fold itself away.

*

Anne and Fargo took Radar for a walk around the block, and when they got back to the room she said she was going to take a bath. "I might have one for the road," he said.

"Get me a glass of something?" she said.

"What would you like?"

"You chose."

"You got it."

He went downstairs, ordered a pint and scanned the wine list.

The bar was quiet, the last diners were drinking coffee, waitresses were wiping down the tables, and the clatter of washing up drifted from the kitchen. Fargo chose a glass of *La Cote Flamenc Picpoul de Pinet Coteaux de Languedoc* from the list, and while he necked his pint, the barmaid said "You're popular."

"Who's popular?"

"You are. And your Mum."

"She's not my Mum."

"No?"

"No."

"Okay, whatever. But you're still popular."

"Says who?"

"There was a bloke here earlier, asking all about you. He was very interested."

"Who was he?"

The barmaid shrugged. "Never seen him before. He was chatting me up, and asked Mary if you were staying…"

"Who's Mary?"

"On reception."

"What did she say?"

"Dunno. He was asking me too."

"What did you say?"

"Nothing. We're not going to tell random strangers who our guests are. Your business is your business, and as long as you don't trash the place, you can do what you like."

"What did he look like?"

"Tall. Thin. I thought he was a copper. Maybe he was, I don't know. Have you been a bad boy?"

Fargo shook his head, finished his pint and picked up the glass of wine. "Not lately," he said.

"You want me to put that on your room?"

"Yeah."

"Okay."

*

One hundred and sixty miles away, Harry Swaine woke up. He didn't feel good. He needed water. He went to the kitchen, ran a tap, splashed his face and filled a glass. He drank deeply, wandered back to the lounge and stared at the carnage. An empty bottle of whisky, spilt rice and curry, empty takeaway boxes, knives and forks and spoons. An upturned table, scattered magazines, a sheet of paper. He picked up the paper and read the invitation he'd written, and the list of names. He shook his head at his stupidity, screwed the sheet into a ball, threw it at the wall, went upstairs and fell on his bed. Two minutes later he was asleep again, and half an hour later he was dreaming about a train. He was trying to catch it, but whenever it was about to arrive in the station, it stopped and went into reverse and trundled back to where it had come from.

He was woken up in the middle of the night by the sound of rain lashing against the window and pouring off the gutters. He sat up and tried to remember where he was and why his head was aching. It didn't take him long.

He lay in the dark and stared at the ceiling. He wasn't tired and his headache had faded, and when the sky lightened he got up, stripped and went to the bathroom. He stood in the shower for twenty minutes, let the water do its thing, soaped his chest, shampooed his hair, rinsed, wrapped himself in towels and went downstairs to make a mug of tea. He drank it in the mess of the living room. Congealed pizza, a half-finished glass of whisky, a scattered newspaper, a road atlas, an upturned vase. A patch of damp in the carpet and the smell of rotten egg. His phone, blinking. He picked it up. He had a message. He listened. He punched redial and when Derek picked up he said "Salisbury?"

"Yes."

"Address?"

Derek told him.

"And they're there now?"

"My colleague tells me they stayed last night, and I haven't heard from him this morning, so I think we can say they probably are."

"Probably?"

"Unless they left very early…"

"Early? They wouldn't know the meaning of the word."

"So what do you want us to do?"

"Send me the bill and leave them to me."

"You sure about that?"

Harry wasn't used to being asked if he was sure about anything. "Just send me the fucking bill," he said, and he hung up, turned his phone off, grabbed his coat and headed outside.

He met Bert by the garage, and told him the news. "Three hours there, three hours back," he said. "See you this afternoon."

Bert smiled. He was wearing a hat Harry hadn't seen before, and over the years, Harry was confident he'd seen every item of clothing Bert owned. He'd seen every checked shirt, every pair of corduroy trousers, and every crusty jacket with patches at the elbow. "Want me to do anything?" he said.

"Yes. Sharpen the chain saw."

"Why?"

"Why?" Harry wasn't used to having his orders answered by a question.

"Yes."

"You seen Scarface?"

"What's Scarface?"

"Oh never mind, Bert. Just do what you have to do," and Harry turned on the radio, put his foot down, sprayed gravel and pointed the Merc west.

*

Fargo had set an alarm for seven o'clock. At eight they were heading down the road to Warminster. The day was grey and wet. They stopped for coffee and bacon rolls at a café on the edge of Salisbury Plain, and as they ate and watched the rain, Anne said "It was always going to be like this. Harry's a jealous man. The moment he knew I was gone, he was looking for me. Or paying someone to look for me."

"Is that what he's done?"

"Of course."

"So how did they find us?"

"Who knows? The car?"

"Maybe we should sell it and catch a train."

Anne shrugged, said "No. I like the old car," and she finished her bacon roll. "That was damn good."

"Better than good," said Fargo, and he finished his. "More coffee?"

"Yes please."

He called the waitress over and ordered, and when she'd gone back to the counter, he said "So if he's got someone looking for us, we need to keep moving."

"We're not doing badly."

"We're doing well. And he's not getting you back, Miss Carter."

"No?"

"Not a chance."

"You're so sweet…"

"I'm not sure about that…"

"I am," she said. "One thing though…"

"What's that?"

"Where's Radar?"

*

Tony Nunn stood behind Salisbury's cow hotel and stared at the space where Anne and Fargo's car had been parked. He stared at the space and he stared at his phone, and he stared at the back of the hotel. The windows were quiet and a blackbird was singing from the roof, singing like a bastard. Tony hadn't had breakfast but he wasn't hungry, though a coffee would have been good. He was going to have a coffee. He liked coffee. He didn't know a lot about coffee but whatever. Black. No sugar. The blackbird did not stop. It sang a beautiful song but in his head it was toast. He liked toast but he preferred a pie. He didn't want a pie. He wanted a coffee. Black. No sugar. He tipped his head back and half wailed. He thought about having a cigarette. He had given up smoking six months before, but now he didn't care. He knew what was coming. It was riding over the horizon with a pen in its mouth and a phone in its hand. He was going to lose his job.

He knocked on the back door of the kitchen. He waited. A porter opened up and said "Yeah?"

"Mary here?"

"Dunno."

Tony Nunn said "I'll find her," pushed past the porter and stepped inside.

Mary was sitting in reception, scrolling through emails. She was tired and hungry, her eyes hurt and she thought she might be pregnant. Her ankles were swollen and she didn't want to be pregnant. She wanted to be in Spain. She wanted to be lying on a beach with a bottle of wine, a doughnut and some tunes. She wanted to be snoozing and she wanted to know that if she wanted she could wander down to the sea and lie down in the water. But she was in Salisbury and it was 8:30 and it was raining and the bloke from last night who asked all the questions about the couple on the top floor was back and looked angry. Mary could do angry, so before he could open his mouth she said "They settled their bill last night, left at half six and no, I don't know where they went. And I don't care. So why don't you just fuck off and leave me alone?"

*

Upstairs, in the room with the view of the roofs and the cathedral spire, Radar snored and dreamt of rabbits. One rabbit was fat and slow, and hopped with a limp. He caught it but when he opened his mouth to eat it, it jumped away and ran into a hole. He looked into the hole and had a good sniff, but instead of smelling rabbit he smelt mince. He opened his eyes and stared across the floor. He could smell too many smells, and some of them were very strange. He heard a mouse scratching in the wall, and birds fidgeting in the eaves. He yawned and stood up and looked towards the bed. It was empty. He lay down again and went back to sleep. It didn't take him long to get back to the rabbits. The fat one was looking out of its hole, its nose twitching, and some smaller ones were standing under a tree he hadn't seen before. Radar liked to sleep and dream, and he liked sausages.

*

Fargo turned the Toyota around and as he drove back to Salisbury, Anne told him about the time she'd suffered from extreme relaxation and left Robert in a hairdressing salon. He'd been two years old and she'd parked him in his pushchair in a quiet corner of the shop, had a wash and then settled in a chair for a cut. "I used to see a lovely chap called Toni. He had a really soothing way about him, and such gentle hands. He used to talk to me about how fine my hair was and how my skin was as clear as a teenager's. He made me feel so happy and relaxed, so when I got up out of the chair I was floating on air and tripped out of the salon without a thought. I was half way home before I realised I was missing something. Even then I wasn't sure what it was – when it hit me I panicked. I ran back to the salon, but I needn't have worried. Robert was chatting away, entertaining Toni and the others."

"So no damage done?"

"Who knows? I sometimes wonder if it had some sort of effect on him. You can never tell what goes on in a baby's head, and what they remember. He's certainly not turned into the sort of man who'd entertain a hairdresser."

"I wonder if leaving Radar on his own is going to turn his head."

"No, I don't think so. I think all we'll have to do is give him a cuddle and a chew."

"Maybe we'll give him two chews."

"That might be an idea."

*

Salisbury's Tony Nunn sat in a café, drank coffee, stared at the ceiling and wondered what had happened. He'd worked for UKTecs for a couple of years, but the army had been his life, and UKTecs wasn't the army. It was business and he wasn't sure he liked business. He wanted bullets and sand and sympathy and flags and women to weep over his boots. And the coffee was bitter. He pushed it away and made a decision. He was going to lose his job, but he didn't care. He didn't care because he was going to resign. He was going to live on his pension. He was going to write a memoir. He'd done his duty. Two tours of Iraq, a divorce, three children he never saw, a one bedroom flat over a betting shop. And he was going to spend more time fishing the chalk streams of Wiltshire and Hampshire, and more time on his allotment. He was going to grow a trio of huge parsnips and win a prize. He stood up, left the café and headed to the office.

He was thinking about the beautiful River Itchen and its banks and reeds as he crossed St John's Street. Was there anything more beautiful than the sight of reeds waving in a gin-clear current on a July morning? A kingfisher, a startled duck, the loop of a perfect cast, a trout persuaded? Maybe. For fifty yards away, something caught his eye and his plans folded themselves away. A Toyota Corolla indicated right and turned into the cow hotel's car park. He wasn't sure if what he was seeing was what he was seeing, but one of the things he'd learned was to always believe your eyes. They never lie. They're your best friends. So he waited for a moment, thought about what he was going to do, decided to put off his resignation for an hour or two, stuffed the parsnip idea in his shoe and headed back the way he'd come. He tucked himself into a doorway and watched as Anne and Fargo parked the car, got out and strolled to the hotel reception. Maybe – he thought – I'm good at this. He took out his phone and called Derek in Canterbury. "Just to let you know," he said, "they're still here. Having a spot of breakfast, I think."

"Okay. The client's on his way. Should be there in an hour or so. Drives a silver Merc. S-class. Big chap. You can't miss him."

"I'll stay in position," said Tony.

"Good man. Let me know if there's any movement."

"Wilco."

*

Fargo rang the bell on the reception desk and when Mary appeared, he said "You won't believe it."

"Try me."

"We forgot the dog."

"You forgot the dog?"

"Yes."

Mary thought this was the funniest thing she'd heard. She put a hand on her tummy, fetched the key and gave it to Anne. Fargo said "We might have a coffee."

"Okay," said Mary, "though you might want to know something."

"Tell me."

"Your friend was asking about you again."

"Which one?"

"The skinny one."

"From the bar?

"Yeah."

"This morning?"

"About half eight."

"What did you tell him?"

"To fuck off."

"And did he?"

"I haven't seen him since."

"Nice one."

"Maybe we'll forget the coffee."

"No, you're all right. He's gone. Take your time. Have it in your room. If I see him, I'll ring up to you."

"Cheers."

"No worries."

Upstairs, Radar was lying on the floor, snoring and dribbling, his legs twitching and his eyeballs rolling behind their lids. He was dreaming about a car and a road and a hedge, and the sun bouncing off a pie. Anne came out of the bathroom. "Okay," said Fargo. "Maybe we should get back on the road. That bloke from last night's been snooping around again."

"And maybe..." said Anne "...we should forget about him and live our own lives."

"That's not a bad idea."

"I'd say it's a damn good idea."

"And how are we going to live?"

"Like this," she said, and she spent an hour showing him in detail, and the detail was easy because there it was and you can take that if you want and put it there, and if that picture looks like a picture it's not because it's a pillow and a song or a ferry, and take that ferry and come back from the island where the rocks grow and sit in that chair if you want but don't get comfortable because I'm falling for you. And that's a mountain or a clock and the telephone line is sagging and take that chicken and put it in the pen and sell her eggs to the man who spends all day outside the shop that never opens on Tuesdays because the woman who runs it likes pancakes and used to live on the moor and collect lampshades. Or was that her brother? I can't remember. But if you've got a moment, could you call the garage about the car because there's something up with the fuel gauge and there's a rattle behind the dashboard that could be a piece of a jigsaw or a domino and then, as they lay in the ruin of the bed he said "Coffee?"

"Yes please."

He got off the bed and padded to the kettle, flicked it on and slapped his stomach.

"Risk it for a biscuit?"

"No thanks."

Radar sat up and growled.

"I need to get some milk," said Fargo.

"Don't worry. I'll have it black."

"Sure?"

"Yes."

"It's no problem."

"Don't worry. Really."

Radar growled again.

"Radar?" she said. "What's the matter?"

"I've never heard him growl," said Fargo.

Anne sat up and looked at the dog. "There's only one person he growls at," she said, and she got out of bed. "Maybe I'll have that coffee later."

"Why?"

"He's called Radar for a reason."

"And what's that?"

"What do you think?" She started to dress.

He watched her and thought the obvious. He didn't need anyone to tell him anything. "I don't know," he said.

"I'd say we've got about ten minutes."

"What are you talking about?"

"Where are my trousers?"

"Here." He picked them up and tossed them onto the bed.

She pulled them on. "Get dressed, Fargo."

"Now?"

"No. In ten minutes. Now!"

"What's going on?"

"Harry's nine minutes away."

"What?"

"Eight and a half."

"How do you know?"

"I don't, but Radar does."

Radar barked.

"He barked," said Fargo. "I've never heard him bark."

"Have you seen him bite?

"No."

"He'll take your leg off."

"Really?"

"Oh yes. He'll take it off and eat it."

"Okay."

They were dressed in two minutes and down the stairs in one. Mary was standing behind reception. "Remembered him this time?" she said.

"Yeah," said Fargo.

"Come on," said Anne.

"Sorry," said Fargo. "We've got to run," and they pushed their way through the back door to the car park. They'd taken a few steps when a voice called "Morning all!" and things started to get busy.

*

The silver Merc had been a comfortable drive, and as he turned onto St John's Street, Harry smiled. He didn't feel tired at all. His eyes were wide, his palms were prickling, and his teeth were on edge. He loved these feelings, the knowledge that control was a posy he held in his hands, and all he had to do was smell it. He slowed, pulled into the cow hotel car park, saw the Toyota Corolla, parked beside it and listened as the engine ticked into silence. Life – he thought – was so sweet, so perfect, and every-thing that came around came around. He had – he could have thought – such a sweet way with a cliché. Driving – he thought – was a good way to spend a morning. Birds riding thermals, fish leaping weirs, horses jumping gates. He whistled through his teeth, rubbed his eyes, opened the car door and stepped out.

He stood by the Toyota for a moment, put his hand on the roof and looked inside. He saw two takeaway coffee cups, a road atlas, a box of tissues and a rucksack. A bag of dog food. A spanner. He considered his options and smiled. The pleasure was almost too much. It rose in him like a golden tower in a field of ripe pigs, and the tower had bells that rang out across a valley of money. He thought for a moment and decided that surprise was the best approach, and likely to provide the most satisfaction. And he wanted satisfaction in fat strings and clots. He wanted to wrap himself in the stuff, and then wrap himself some more. So he got back in the Merc, backed it into the street, parked, strolled back to the hotel and sat at a smoker's table on a covered patio. He was hidden from view but could see everything – the back and side doors of the hotel, the street, the entrance to the car park, the roofs of houses, the Toyota. He wasn't usually a patient man but sitting and waiting there was easy and a grand way to spend an hour or so. But he didn't have to wait an hour. Two minutes later, the back door opened and Fargo appeared, Anne behind him, Radar behind her. He stood up, shouted "Morning all!" and things started to get busy.

Fargo was first. He didn't care. He was feeling fit and strong and hungry, and as Harry stepped out from behind the table, he said "What you doing here, fat man?"

"I've come for my wife," said Harry, but that was one of the last things he said that morning because Radar, fortified by a knotted rawhide chew and a good snooze, and recognising the man as the bastard who'd never fed him and had kicked him on more than one occasion, launched himself with an enthusiastic yelp, grabbed an arm and dug in. His old teeth found bone and once they'd done that, they started to grind, and as Harry screamed and tried to beat the hound away, Anne took a swing with her handbag, a heavy Louis Vuitton with a substantial buckle. She caught him on the side of the head, swung again and caught him on the cheek. Splattered and frenzied by the smell of blood, Radar started shaking his head back and forth, Fargo grabbed the dog's collar and pulled, but this made things worse. The teeth locked, Harry wailed, Mary came running from reception, and Tony Nunn, who'd been watching from a corner of the car park, hesitated. Mary held her belly and yelled "What the fuck's going on?"

"It's okay!" said Anne.

"Like hell it is," said Mary. For a moment she thought she was going to have her baby. It kicked and felt like it wanted to sing a song, maybe something by that bloke out of Morbid Angel. "I'm calling the cops." She felt some bile rising, trickling into her mouth. It pooled on her tongue and then started to trickle back down again.

"No!" yelled Fargo.

"Call them!" screamed Harry.

Mary retched and disappeared.

Anne hit Harry again, this time full in the face. The buckle on the bag caught his nose with a fine crunch, and as blood poured from his ruptured nostrils, he reached down and punched Radar in the mouth. The shock of the punch made the dog lose his grip and Fargo yanked him away. Harry straightened and twisted to the right as Anne took another swing, this time with her foot. She caught him a perfect punt between the legs and as he went down, blinded by blood and howling with pain, she turned and walked away. "Come on, boys," she said, "we've got places to go," and she headed towards the Toyota.

Tony Nunn hesitated for another moment, then made his move. His move lasted ten seconds. Anne saw him and said "Want to ask the dog some questions?" Radar growled and strained against his collar.

"Er... no..."

"Thought not," and then they were in the car, backing it out, spinning into the road and away, and when Harry tried to follow them he walked into the edge of the swinging back door, split his forehead, tripped and fell face down into a bucket of sand, rainwater and fag ends.

*

Radar sat in the back of the car, licking his lips and making the occasional low bark. "I think he enjoyed that," said Fargo.

"I think we all did," said Anne. "Apart from my poor bag." She took out some tissues, spat on them and started to clean it. "You wouldn't have thought he'd cut so easily."

"Bullies always do. And bleed like pigs."

"He is a pig."

They were out of the city, cruising down the road to Andover. They'd decided to head east, reasoning that Harry or anyone else would expect them to head west. "He might think the same as us," said Fargo. "Double-bluff the double-bluffer..."

"No," said Anne. "He's not that clever."

"Sure about that?"

"Oh yes. He might be a good businessman, but have you ever met a businessman with a brain?"

"I thought it was important to have one."

She shook her head. "Not important at all. Greed, selfishness, the ability to count, an inability to empathise..."

They drove in silence for a few minutes, watching the clouds and the rain and the sodden fields. The car smelt of iron and cabbage. After a few miles, they took a minor road and headed north, drove into a small village and parked down a side road. They sat for a couple of minutes and listened to the rain.

"I need some air."

"Me too."

"Come on."

Five minutes later they were sitting in a pub at a window table, ordering coffee and watching the road. The view was obscured by a tree growing from a circle of grass, a vintage plough and a wheelie bin, and as they waited for the drinks, the rain did that thing when it suddenly intensifies and blows against the glass, and streams ran down the verges and puddled into lakes in the middle of the road.

"Jesus," said Anne.

"Yeah," said Fargo and he reached across and picked up the menu, read it, put it back and sighed a long sigh that sounded like a door closing by itself.

*

Back at Salisbury's cow hotel, the police had been called, and following a professional analysis of the situation, PC Steven Eliot and his colleague WPC Joanna Blackburn concluded that at this point in time there was not a great deal they could do as it was basically a domestic issue going forward, and even though Mr Swaine wasn't interested in pressing charges, they would give him a number to call and if he changed his mind about things they would be happy to discuss his options there and then. He told them that they weren't to hold their breath and this pleased them, because they were busy with other things anyway. PC Eliot had spent most of the morning trying and failing to download a fitness app to his phone, and WPC Blackburn was worried about cheesecake. The app could tell him what sort of exercise he was doing. Cycling, running, walking, swimming – it was amazing. WPC Blackburn's cheesecake issue involved a rogue slice she'd eaten the previous evening. She'd calculated that it contained at least 400 calories, and she'd need to run for at least 30 minutes to burn 400 calories, and the more she thought about these numbers the more anxious she got. And when she got anxious she got depressed, and when she got depressed she looked to comfort in chips, wine and a fantasy that involved PC Eliot, who she loved more than her husband. With his beautiful chin and the calm and patient way he spoke to people, and his blue eyes and the little curly hairs that grew between his knuckles, he was the perfect colleague. And the more she thought about his chin the more she realised that her life was a mess, and as they drove away from the hotel, she bit her lip and wanted to be swimming across an infinity pool towards two glasses.

As he watched the police car disappear, Harry cupped his chin and moved it from one side to the other, and said "So you're the town's man of the moment?" to Tony.

Tony was feeling sore. Somehow he'd managed to strain his right shoulder, and if there was one part of his body he really didn't want to strain, it was his right shoulder. A right handed fly fisherman needs his right shoulder. He took a step towards Harry and stared at the fat man's face. It was a mess. His nose looked broken, his top lip was split and drying blood was smeared across his chin. His shirt was torn and as he breathed he made a heavy sound, like a barn door creaking at a horse. "You really need to clean yourself up," said Tony.

"You think so?" said Harry.

Tony took another step forward and something rose in him, a needle of heat and anger and frustration. "Yes," he said. "I do."

Harry shook his head.

"Are you saying you don't?"

Harry recognised something in Tony's voice, something dangerous and black. Both men twitched, and on the far side of the car park a leaf dropped off a tree, curled in the air and landed on a dustbin.

"You're a mess, and not just to look at," said Tony.

Harry clenched his fists and planted his feet.

"Before I picked up this job, I read your file. Your wife's run off with the gardener. Makes you wonder. All very M'Lady and Mellors, wouldn't you say?"

"What?"

"You know. D.H. Lawrence?"

"No," said Harry. "I don't know. And I don't care," and he took a poor swing at Tony who stepped to one side, avoided the fist, clipped the fat man on the back of his off-balance head and walked away. He didn't look back but he didn't care. He'd seen birds eat human brains. He was going fishing and later he was going to drink beer from a bottle, tip his head back and count the clouds.

*

Anne and Fargo finished their coffee, took Radar for a stroll in the rain, then sat in the car and thumbed an atlas. "Okay," he said.

"Okay," she said.

"You still on for Wales?"

"Of course." She leaned across and leant her head on his shoulder. She closed her eyes. She felt warm and safe. "Why do you smell of tar?" she said.

"I don't know."

"It's such a good smell. A real smell."

"I'm glad you like it."

"I love it."

"And I love this." He patted the steering wheel.

"Good."

He closed the atlas and dropped it onto the floor behind his seat. "We've got a few miles to go."

"That's true."

"So let's get going."

*

Derek sat in his office with a cup of coffee, a digestive biscuit and his view of Canterbury cathedral, and once he'd checked his emails he called Tony. Tony looked at the ringing phone, noted the name and thought about ignoring it. He could ignore it now and he could ignore it later, but eventually he'd have to answer it, so he did what he had to do and told Derek that things had gone tits up in a wheelbarrow. He thought about saying that he didn't care and was going fishing, but stopped himself.

"How?"

"Well, the targets are travelling with a dog."

"I know."

"Have you seen it?"

"Have I seen what?"

"The dog."

"No. Why?"

"Put it this way, it's not Lassie. And it doesn't like the client. Sorry, correction. It likes the client very much. As a mid-morning snack."

"What happened?"

Tony explained, and as he did, Derek felt his colleague's despondency jump the miles from Salisbury and settle in the office. A dark pointlessness about what he was doing, and a uselessness. For what were they doing and why were they doing it? Helping a bully find the woman he beat so he could beat her some more? When he was a police officer at least he did some good some of the time – now all he did was agitate sin. He was a paddle in the sewer but he supposed it paid the bills and the bills needed paying, and the kids needed their school trips and Rachel needed to pay their neighbour to fix the leak in the roof and he needed to put some aside for a holiday or the deposit on a new car so he pushed all qualms to one side, and when Tony finished by telling him that Mr Swaine had laughed at the suggestion he visit A&E and had cleaned himself up in the hotel toilets before getting back in his car and heading back the way he'd come, he said "So any idea where the targets are?"

"None at all. They could be anywhere. Who knows?"

"So we're back to square one."

"It looks that way."

"Great," said Derek, and once he'd absorbed this truth, he said "Well, thanks for what you did. I don't think they'll be heading your way again, so you can cross them off your list."

"Already done," said Tony.

"And if you're ever this way, call in for a drink. It'd be good to meet."

"I don't think that's going to happen."

"No?"

"No. I'm going fishing, Derek, and I don't think I'll be coming back."

"Fishing? Is that a metaphor for something?"

"I've never done metaphor," said Tony, "and I don't intend to start now."

*

Harry swore as he drove and he ached, and when he stopped for a cup of coffee and the waitress looked at his cuts and the dried blood on his face and said "You all right, love?" he grunted and said "No I'm fucking not."

"Anything I can do?"

He looked her up and down and thought about it. There probably was but he didn't have the time, so he said "Yeah. Fetch my coffee and then fuck off."

"Charming," she said.

Two minutes later, the waitress's boss, a bad-tempered Scotsman with nostrils full of wire and hands the size of bibles, came from the back office, said "You the one with the foul mouth?"

"Who's asking?" said Harry.

"Me and me brother."

"Big lad, is he?"

"Big enough for you."

"Oh, no. I think I just pissed myself."

"Hamish!"

A door opened and a man appeared who made the boss look frail. Harry shook his head with the weariness of someone who wants coffee but sees nothing but tea, and started to stand up. He was halfway out of his seat when Hamish put a hand on his shoulder, took a grip and pushed down. Harry didn't like to be touched but knew he had no choice. He felt rage building and he looked at Hamish and Hamish looked back, and then he was suddenly overwhelmed by a sensation he didn't recognise, a crushing that gave him a sharp headache and the feeling he was lost and everything was hopeless. A weakness swept through him, and when he opened his mouth to say something nothing came out.

"What's the matter?" said Hamish. "Not so good at bullying men?"

Harry felt his tongue in his mouth but there was nothing he could do with it. It lay in there like a fish. He shook his head, slowly.

"Okay," said Hamish. "You've got a choice. You can get up, turn around, leave our place, get in your car and drive away, or you can get up and come round the back."

Harry opened his mouth again but still nothing came. He felt confused and lost and the ache in his head became a stabbing. The confusion turned to something like panic and he started to sweat. He wondered what was round the back and whether he'd be able to handle it. He didn't wonder long. He knew he had to leave, and as he stood up and took the short walk from the table to the café door, his legs felt like rain. He'd never experienced this sort of humiliation, this shame and loss and pain, and he wasn't sure how to behave. Should he try and walk tall and proud or simply slink away like the likely cat? He didn't know. And as he stepped outside into real rain, and Hamish gave him a gentle push in his back, and the waitress called "See ya!" he thought he heard church bells pealing in his head, huge bells ringing out towards a dirty horizon and on, past whatever view was waiting for him.

*

Less than fifty miles away, the road was slow, clogged with rain and caravans and squalls. Radar dozed and Anne listened to a discussion on the radio. Some people were talking about their lives, the books they'd read and the politics of climate change. A rock star had just returned from the Arctic where he'd climbed a mountain on Greenland and looked down at a dusty valley. "This time last year," he said, "it was a glacier," and he said he'd witnessed scenes of environmental degradation in Indonesia, Australia, Fiji, Brazil, Ghana and Ireland. In fact, wherever he went, he met with disaster, and he was starting to wonder if the game was already up. "We have to learn from our mistakes, understand that unless we do something now, it's over." A novelist underlined the point by saying that she had had the same thoughts the last time she visited Peru and a latest trip to India and Nepal with a stop-over in Thailand on the way to Australia and New Zealand had confirmed it . "People are dying," she said, "so we can enjoy cheap flights to wherever…" Fargo said "Can we listen to some tunes?"

"Of course."

"What do you fancy?"

"Surprise me."

He scrolled his phone and chose something, and as the music filled the car, Anne closed her eyes and tried to enjoy it. She almost understood it and tapped her foot in time, and after a couple of minutes said "This is good for driving."

"Driving, dancing, chilling, you name it…"

"Who is it?"

"Mr Scruff."

"Sounds like a good name for a dog."

"He's not a dog," said Fargo, and suddenly they met a queue of traffic, the road dropped and to the right, squatting in the damp, grey and green, corralled by wire and stared at by knots of bewildered visitors, they saw Stonehenge.

"Stonehenge!" she said. "I forgot it was here."

"Easily done. You seen it before?"

"Once. When I was a kid."

"Want to stop?"

"I don't know. Should we?"

"I'll buy you a fridge magnet."

"Oh. My first present…"

He smiled and leaned towards her and said "I'll give you a present."

"I bet you will."

*

Derek left his office and strolled into Canterbury town centre. He usually ate a sandwich and an apple at his desk, but today he was going to treat himself to fish and chips. He owed himself. He'd read somewhere that you should buy yourself a present every day, and this was one of the keys to happiness. Or contentment. Or ease. Or something. He wasn't big on philosophy, but he did have some beliefs. For example, he believed you should take a walk every day, never read newspapers, and resist the temptation to grow a beard. And if you find a screw or nail in the road, you should pick it up and drop it down the first drain you see. Then you'll never get a puncture, either in a tyre or your life.

The streets were busy, and when he reached his favourite pub he stepped inside, took a deep breath, went up to the bar and smiled at the woman behind the pumps. He recognised her and she recognised him.

"Hey," she said. "How's it going?"

"Good. You?"

"I'm lovely."

"I can see that," he said.

"Oh please. Pint?"

"Yes please."

"Any preference?"

He scanned the pumps. "Surprise me."

"You got it."

While she poured, he scanned the menu and changed his mind about the fish and chips. Every now and again he liked to surprise himself twice, so he ordered a venison and sloe gin pie with new potatoes, beans and carrots, found a table with a view of the cathedral gate and sat back to drink and watch the tourists.

The tourists weren't bothered by the rain. They loved it and they loved the old buildings, the narrow streets, the high roofs, the shops and the idea that soon they'd be having a cup of tea in a café where Shakespeare used to spend his afternoons before going home to write one of his films. Some had arrived in the city as members of a coach party and others were travelling independently. There were single people and couples, and families with young children, and there were people who knew exactly where they were, and others who thought they were in Lincoln. There were dog lovers and stamp collectors, alcoholics, violinists, retired surgeons, resting actors and students who smelt of yeast. Lens polishers and drivers. Some were from France and Germany, and others had come from China.

A couple from Russia came into the pub as the waitress brought Derek his food, and as he thanked her and said "No thanks" when she asked if he wanted any sauces, they took photographs of the bar. They had big cameras and heavy coats, and their shoes clipped on the floor and the floor clipped back, and as Derek cut his pie and the steam rose, his phone rang. He picked it up and looked at the screen, stared at the words "Brenda's mobile", let it go through to messages and then turned it off. If today's present to himself was an unusual pie, he was wrapping it in an undisturbed hour and tying it with a ribbon made of rumination. And if the office was burning down and Brenda was trapped in a cupboard, then there was nothing he could do about it anyway, so he might as well sit back and enjoy the view, the glossy cobbles and the smell of hops. And even though the sound of a distant fire engine made him wonder, he dismissed any thoughts that would bother his hour, and speared a potato with his fork, popped it in his mouth and chewed.

*

Anne and Fargo stood in the rain and stared at Stonehenge. They had been disappointed by the range of fridge magnets available in the crumbling visitor centre, appalled by the squalid under-pass that led to the site, disturbed by the constant rumble of traffic, and unnerved by the patrolling security. As they stood beside a rope and stared at the stones, Fargo said "They've been switched off."

"What do you mean?"

"Well, maybe they were once alive, you know, had some sort of power that gave people energy or something, but they're not working any more. They're just a pile of old stones. No one cares about them, however much people say they do."

"The druids love them."

"Yeah, but they're not real druids. I read about them. You could write everything we know about the real druids on the back on a postcard. Those people are traffic wardens dressed in sheets. Okay, so they spend the night singing songs and chanting stuff and hitting drums and pretending they're getting in touch with trees, but they're fooling themselves. And for everyone else, this place is just another thing to look at for twenty minutes before having a cup of tea and a piece of cake."

"If I didn't know you better, I'd say you were a cynic."

"But it's the truth, isn't it?"

"Maybe."

"I'm not saying they don't look amazing. It's just that they're switched off. Maybe even dead."

They walked on, squelching through the grass and mud, and although the sun was obscured by grim, lowering cloud, and drizzle layered across the desperate plain, and a line of transport planes roared overhead, and crows waited on the broken fence posts that trailed barbed wire towards the horizon before slowly spreading their wings and taking off one after another, lifting into the rain, banking right and lancing towards the west; although these things conspired to layer the early afternoon with a feeling of doom, there was no doom in Anne or Fargo's hearts. The pale ghosts of the day faded and there was happiness in their eyes, and anticipation, and on their way back to the car they stopped at the shop and he did what he'd promised and bought her a present.

*

When Derek got back to his office, there were three Post-it notes stuck to his computer screen. He peeled them off and pinched them between his fingers. He tried to remember how he'd coped before the invention of Post-it notes. He often did this sort of thing, just allowing his mind to wander to a sepia past. He closed his eyes. The notes felt like nothing and he hoped they were. He opened his eyes. The first read "Your wife called." The second "Call MacGregor." MacGregor was his boss in the London office. The third read "Tried to call. I've gone for lunch. Back at 2:30. B."

Derek looked at his watch. It was 2:15. He turned on his phone and put it on the desk. A minute later it buzzed and the screen told him he had four missed calls and six texts. He woke his computer and a dozen emails dropped into his inbox. The phone in Brenda's office starting to ring. He tipped back in his chair and closed his eyes again and wondered the thing he wondered every day: "How have we come to this?" and as the words turned in his head he tried to remember the last time he'd sent a postcard. He wasn't sure, but he thought it was probably ten years before, when he and Rachel and the kids had holidayed in Greece, on the island of Kefallinia, where they'd stayed in an apartment in Fiskardho, a place with its own terrace and views of the harbour and distant Ithaki. The day before they'd left for this holiday his mother had complained of feeling unwell; he thought she was inventing a malaise because she didn't want them to be away for two weeks, so he made her promise to see the doctor and promised to send a postcard. A picture of a donkey on a dusty, yellow road, a Greek couple in traditional dress standing next to the animal, he smoking, she holding a basket of lemons. "Dear Mother," he wrote on the back, "We're all enjoying hot weather and plenty of good food. The fish is very good. The children are enjoying swimming in some of the clearest sea you can imagine. Hope all's well with you, Much love, Derek." He didn't know if she ever read the last postcard he ever wrote; when they arrived home it was to the news that she had died in her sleep two nights previously.

He picked up the phone and dialled home. Rachel answered with a breathless voice, as if she'd been running up and down the stairs all morning. "Oh hi, darling," she said.

"You called."

"I did. Could you pick up some paracetamol on the way home."

"Paracetamol?"

"Yeah."

"Is that all?"

"I think so."

"Have you got a headache?"

"Not any more."

Derek thought about this for a moment, then thought that he might be getting a headache himself. "Okay," he said. "See you later…" and he hung up. A minute later he called his boss, who answered with a bad-tempered "MacGregor…" and said that he'd had a call from the police in Salisbury, where a client who was traced back to the Canterbury office had been involved in a fracas with Tony from the Salisbury office.

"Know anything about this?"

"Probably know more than you. He's a butcher…"

"And what's that got to do with the price of shovels?"

"He's a butcher and his wife's gone off with the gardener."

MacGregor snorted. A snort was as close to a laugh as MacGregor got to a laugh.

"So they got in a car and drove to Salisbury, and when I informed the client, he was down there in a shot, kicking off in a pub car park."

"Classy."

"Oh he's a lovely chap."

"Case closed?"

"We're not sure."

"Let me know," said MacGregor, and he hung up.

*

Harry drove in a haze of fury and pain and confusion, replaying the day's events, examining them, turning them like pancakes, trying to work them out, looking at the burnt edges and the bits that hadn't cooked properly. He took deep breaths and filled his lungs, and he tasted the smell. He didn't like it. He gagged. He swallowed. He tasted so bad. He understood what had happened but couldn't understand how he'd let such a simple job spiral. You find your wife, you beat her lover, you haul her home, you slap her, push her in the bedroom, take her phone, lock the door and put the key in your pocket. Eight steps to resolution. What could be easier?

He couldn't remember a time when he hadn't been in control. From making sure his younger brother always did exactly as he was told, to manipulating his mother into acquiescing to all his demands, to blackmailing his teachers into giving him top marks, to tricking his father into giving him fifteen thousand pounds, to persuading Anne to give up a promising career as a Cordon Bleu chef de partie. He supposed that the only important thing he'd been unable to control had been Michael's sexual orientation, and even though bullying the boy for a couple of years and then throwing him out of the house had given him a degree of satisfaction, he was still out there, contaminating the world and dragging the name of Swaine through the gutter. But he had plans. He always had plans. They turned in his head like chickens on a spit, dripping their fat into a tray, slowly turning to gold. And when he thought about what he was going to do next, he felt his haze of fury fade and weaken, and the road opened up like a feast. Women to serve eight or nine courses, all the drink you could manage and all the drink you couldn't, and dogs to snap at the scraps.

*

As Fargo drove, Anne dabbed at the Stonehenge summer meadow lip balm he'd bought her, held it to her nose and smiled, and as her smile spread she felt her eyes water, and as her eyes watered, an obvious feeling broke in her heart, and as the cracks spread across the beating muscle, she let her smile give itself a laugh. The day had had its moments but now, as they drove into a clearing west and the sun peeled holes in the clouds, she felt happy and optimistic, and wondered when she'd last felt happy or optimistic. This wondering seemed to defeat the purpose of feeling happy and optimistic, so she stopped wondering and allowed herself to sink into the idea that a new life could open its arms and take her somewhere precious. And when she thought about the word "precious" she liked the feeling, and the way the word sounded like a wave dragging shingle down a secret beach.

And as he drove, Fargo looked at Anne. Her eyes were closed and her hair waved in the draught from the car's vents, and he wondered what she was smiling about, but didn't ask. He could guess and his guess would probably be right, but even if it was wrong he wouldn't care.

The road passed through a tunnel of trees and climbed to a place where it crested the top of a hill, and a lay-by offered a view of the distant north and west. Fargo pulled in, parked and said "Fancy a Mr Whippy?" An ice cream van was parked at the far end of the lay-by.

"Why not?" said Anne.

They climbed out of the car and while Radar ran off for a sniff, they walked to the van, bought two ice creams, considered the flake option, decided to do the right thing and strolled down a path that led to a circle of heath and a bench.

They sat down to lick and crunch, and Radar sat down to watch and hope. The holes in the clouds grew ragged and wide, and beams of sunlight broke onto the land, and in the distance, the Severn estuary shone like a spiv's cravat. Beyond its cut, the hills of Wales faded into the horizon. Fargo pointed and said "That's where we're going…" and then "Thank you."

"Thank you? For what?"

"I'm not sure. Everything, I suppose."

She took his hand and squeezed it. "When I met you, I never thought you'd turn out to be a romantic."

"No?"

"Certainly not."

"So did I?"

"Did you what?"

"Turn out to be a romantic."

"Yes," she said.

"And is that a good thing?"

"Of course it is."

Below them, a magpie broke cover, then another. He saluted them and then said "I'm not sure what to say."

"If you're not sure, say nothing. Always a good policy."

"Okay."

*

In Broadstairs, Bert heard the growl of Harry's car, hauled himself out of the armchair in the shed and picked up the chain saw. He wasn't sure why he'd be asked to sharpen it but he'd done as he'd been told. He weighed it in his hand. He didn't ask questions. It wasn't heavy. He always did as he was told. It was ready to go, twinkling with grease and oil.

He negotiated the sacks and wood and string and tools that littered the shed floor, shouldered the door and sniffed. The shed smelt of grass and petrol. This was a smell he liked, and sometimes he wondered if he preferred it to the smell of fresh air. And sometimes he didn't. And sometimes, mostly, he didn't care.

He shuffled down the path between the vegetables and the plum tree wall, and when he reached the low door that led to the yard, he stopped and watched. Harry parked and sat for a moment before climbing out of the car and leaning against its roof. Bert wheezed and the noise made Harry look up. He snarled "What you looking at?"

"Sir…"

"What?"

"I…"

"Yes?"

"I… I sharpened it."

"You did what?"

"The chain saw. You asked me to."

"Oh Jesus..." Harry said, and he waved his hand at the old man, turned and went for the back door.

Bert had seen his boss in poor states but he'd never seen him look as bad – his face was bruised and blood was crusted in his nostrils, and his jacket sleeves were ripped. He walked with a limp and stumbled when he reached the door. He slipped his keys and when he tried to pick them up dropped them again and ended up on his knees, his head resting against the threshold. Bert propped the chain saw against a boot scraper and took a step, but before he could get any further Harry put a hand up and hissed "Go, Bert. Just go..."

"Sir..."

"No..."

"But I..."

"Bert ! Fuck off! Just fuck off home..."

Now Bert was loyal and he respected Harry, but if anything killed respect it was the use of profanities. And a word like that, directed at him, it was disgraceful. He hadn't fought in the war to be told to do that. He stared at Harry and Harry knew but didn't care – he waved a hand again and found his keys and found the lock and the handle and opened the door, and when it swung open he fell inside and lay on the floor for a moment before hauling himself up and staggering down the corridor to the kitchen, the fridge and a beer.

Bert had seen enough. He took the chain saw back to the shed, locked the door, took his bicycle from its place and wheeled it down the path to the bottom gate. Then he cycled into town and had decided to pick up some fish and chips to eat at home but changed his mind and stopped for a pint in Neptune's Hall, a pub. He'd never been a big drinker but some days the choice was made for you. And once he'd settled at a table and smelt the pie and mash, he decided to eat. And once he'd eaten and had another pint, he started talking to the woman who sat at the next table, sipping a G&T and scrolling through her phone.

Normally Bert was discrete. He wouldn't talk to a stranger about his boss, wouldn't gossip or tell anyone what he thought about his boss's wife and her lover boy, but there was something about the woman and her very blue eyes and the concerned way she leant her head towards him when he felt the beer tip him over the edge and force him to say "You know Harry Swaine?"

"I'm not sure," she said. "I've heard the name, but…"

"He's the biggest butcher… the biggest butcher in Kent."

"Beat our meat?"

"That's the one. All the sausages you can eat. Famous, he is."

"Of course he is."

"Had one of those ads on the telly."

"I remember it."

"He's my boss."

"Is he?"

"Was a few hours ago. Good bloke. I know him. Yeah…" Bert looked into his glass. "Well, thought I did. But then his missus… she… what does she just go and do?"

The woman's eyes widened but Bert didn't notice. He was focused on the bottom of his glass. It was almost empty.

"You look like you need another," said the woman.

"You buying?"

"For a gentleman like you, of course."

"Bert," said Bert.

"Nice to meet you, Bert. I'm Abigail. Abi."

"Hello Abi."

"And what's that?" She pointed at his glass.

"Spitfire," he said. "The bottle of Britain."

Abi clicked her fingers, pointed at the glass and the barman pulled.

"So you were saying. Your boss and his wife…"

"He ought to show her his hand. Tell her what's what."

The barman put the pint in front of Bert, Abi paid for it and said "Sounds like she's done something pretty bad."

"Oh yes," said Bert, and he took a long pull on the pint. "The whore. Excuse me…"

"Please," she said. "I'm a woman of the world."

"Went off with the gardener, didn't she? Even took the dog. Broke his heart. Not that he'd want anyone to know that." He put a finger to his lips and leant towards her. "He doesn't want anyone to know anything about it. Proud man, my boss. Wouldn't want people to think he couldn't control his missus, would he?"

"Of course he wouldn't," said Abi. "You wouldn't want anyone to think you couldn't control yours, would you?"

"Not married," said Bert.

"Well, I'm sure that if you were," said Abi, and she leaned forward and put a gentle hand on his arm, "that you wouldn't."

Bert thought about that, tried to work out exactly what he should say, and then nodded. "Suppose so," he mumbled and took another swig.

"So," said Abi. "Harry's wife…"

"Anne. Anne Swaine…"

"Of course."

"She and the gardener…"

"No," said Bert, and he jabbed his chest. "I shouldn't have said he was the gardener. I'm the gardener. He was just the lad."

"Of course."

"Pushed a barrow. That's all Fargo was good for."

"Fargo?"

"Yes. Stupid name isn't it?"

"It is unusual. And they've taken off with each other?"

"They have. Took the car. I reckon the boss has been all over looking for them. Came home today all battered and bruised…"

"Did he?"

"Looked like he'd been in a fight."

"And he still lives at… er… that house…"

"He does. Hyde Hall."

"Of course. Hyde Hall," said the woman, and then "Would you excuse me a minute. I just need to find the loo. Don't go anywhere…"

"Of course not," said Bert, and he watched as she stood up and made her way to the back of the pub where she took out a notebook and wrote "Harry Swaine, Anne, Fargo gardener, dog, Hyde Hall…" in a list. Her memory wasn't what it used to be, and she was thinking about having another drink, and she couldn't trust herself to remember a thing.

*

Anne and Fargo and Radar didn't stop again until they'd crossed the river Severn and were in Abergavenny. It was half eight and the streets were filling with the young people of the town. Boys were racing their cars, girls were gathering in bunches, music was booming from the open doors of pubs, a police car was cruising. The evening light was thick with water and when the first street lights flickered on they cast an echo of the rumbles to come. They found a hotel on the main street and were given a big bedroom with a view of rooftops and the Black Mountains, and after a drink and a plate of pasta, they got an early night. The day had been long and hard and too exciting, and now they were in Wales they thought they would be free to sleep a long night.

As they lay in bed, the sounds of the town lulled them to sleep – revving cars, booming music, yelling women and their bullying men. Everything usual and comforting, like the sheets they lay on and the light that beat through the cracks in the curtain. But at half past five, Anne suddenly woke from a dream. It had started quietly enough – she'd been sitting on a cliff, looking down at a jumble of colourful but rusting machines. One of them was an Apollo space capsule, and as she stared at it, it began to change and stretch and become a small ship with tall masts and white sails. She was invited aboard by a man in a smart uniform, and he sailed the ship away from the jumble of machines to a steaming jungle where it docked at a small pier. She disembarked and started walking up a path, and as she walked she knew she was going to get lost. Birds were calling from the high trees, and crawling creatures were rustling through the undergrowth. In the dream she wasn't afraid but she was nervous and the backs of her legs ached. The path was narrow and started to climb a hill. She reached a plateau. She walked to the edge and looked down. The drop was sheer and running with water, and she knew that she was almost lost, so she turned around and walked back the way she'd come. After a mile or so, she saw a door, opened it and found herself in the lobby of what appeared to be an old school or university. She walked across the lobby. There was a beautiful mural on the wall, and the sound of people laughing. She stepped into a sunlit courtyard, and at that moment knew she wasn't lost. The people laughing were Robert and Mike, her sons. They were sharing a bottle of wine and when they saw her, they both jumped up and ran towards her. And that was when she woke up and sat up, and stared at the curtains.

Dawn light illuminated the room, spreading slowly like water in a rising flood. The street was quiet and the parties were done.

Radar snuffled. She looked down at Fargo. He was sleeping on his back, his head turned towards her, his hair spread like a rash across the pillow. She reached out and stroked his face. He was cool and beautiful and strong, and the years stretched out in front of him. So he'd made mistakes but everyone makes mistakes and he would do good things too, maybe even something great. Or maybe not. Whatever. There was plenty of time for him. And she thought about her years, diminishing, fading and poor, and she looked at the back of her hand. The veins were stringy, the skin was starting to mottle and thin. She looked at her arm, at the loose flesh and the spots, and she looked at her bulging stomach and the more she stared the more she wondered why. Why was he lying with her when he could be lying with a young thing from the pub across the road? Why was he risking his future with a lonely wash-up? So he'd told her that she was different, but wasn't everyone different? Wasn't that the thing that made us human? Or at least one of the things. So was he just looking for the mother he'd lost, or was he afraid to say no? Or worse, did he simply feel sorry for her? And the more the questions came, the paler she felt. Sleep wasn't going to come again, not for a while anyway, so she slipped a leg out of bed, then another, padded across the room, picked up her clothes and went to the bathroom.

She stared at her face in the mirror and realised it was worse than she'd thought. The lines and wrinkles and creases she'd always dreaded looked like more than evidence of her age or experience or whatever word people used to try and sooth the inevitable – they looked like scars and wounds, and the closer she looked the worse they seemed. And her hair – once it had been rich and brown and full. Now it was thin and grey was showing through, dead grass on a rock. She took a deep, sighing breath and the inescapable tapped her shoulder and whispered in her ear. There was no turning at the crossroads. No looking at some horizon and no shining glass. The decision was made. She dressed quickly.

Half an hour later, she slipped out of the hotel and headed down the main street. Radar padded beside her, his big head lolling, confused by the hour. The pavements were littered with the ruins of the night – bottles, polystyrene boxes, cans, socks and empty fag packets. She followed the signs to the railway station, away from the bus station and up the road past neat little houses and their gardens. A cat arched. The first car of the morning, a taxi. High above her, an aeroplane laid its trail in thin, freezing air. When she reached the station, she checked the times. The next southbound train was due in five minutes. She'd be in Cardiff at 7:50, and there'd be plenty of trains to London. She could be home by lunch, and then all she had to do was take the bruises and be the woman she'd always been and always would be.

*

Fargo woke to the sound of rain beating against the window, turned over and stretched out his arm. When he reached out and didn't feel Anne's body, he sat up and looked around the room. The bathroom door was closed. He called her name. When she didn't reply he decided she was busy doing the things a woman does in the morning, dropped his head back on the pillow, closed his eyes and dozed.

Half an hour later, he woke again. He didn't have to sit up and look around to know that something wasn't right. But when he did, he saw the bathroom door still closed, half the bed cold, Radar gone, Anne's bag gone, silence. A folded sheet of paper on the table by the window. He got up and read:

Dear Fargo,

I'm sorry, but I can't do this any more. Please don't hate me, but when I woke up I looked at you and you were sleeping so peacefully, and you know what I realised when I was there? It was quite simple, really, but I have to tell you. I have to stop this now, because if I don't one of us will, sooner or later. Of course. I mean, what are you thinking? You don't need to spend your time with an old bird like me. I know you've told me that I'm special, and I have tried to believe you, but really I know you're just sorry for me, aren't you? And that's very sweet of you and you know I'll never forget how kind and lovely you've been, but now it's my turn to be kind to you, and let you go. So I'm taking Radar and my stuff, but I'll leave you the car, and you'll find a couple of thousand pounds in your bag. So you can go to that place in Wales and buy yourself all the ice cream you want, and get a job and live the sort of life you deserve with a pretty girl your own age. You're so lovely and it's been an adventure, but this isn't real. We can't live like we're in a film or something. And please don't try to follow me – I can find my own way back. I'll never forget you, Fargo.

With lots of love, and thank you,
Anne x

He dropped the letter, dressed and was out of the room four minutes later. He ran downstairs, scared the receptionist by yelling "Where is she!", got no answer, ran into the street and almost knocked a cyclist off his bike. He yelled her name – "Anne! Anne!" and when he got no answer, he ran back into the hotel, went to the room, splashed cold water on his face, threw his stuff into his bag and went back down to pay the bill.

"I'm sorry," he said, counting tenners. "My girlfriend left…"

"Your girlfriend?" said the receptionist. "We thought she was your mother."

Fargo shook his head. "No," he hissed. "She was... is... she is my girlfriend."

"Okay, okay. Jeez. Keep your hair on..."

"And you keep the change," he said, tossing the last tenner at the receptionist, and then he was out and running around the side of the hotel to the car park and the Toyota and the road south.

*

Abigail Grey didn't think she was a failure, but she did feel unfulfilled. She'd always wanted to be a journalist, a campaigner writing stories that made a difference. Serious stories that underlined her compassion and desire to see a fairer world. But the years had passed, she'd missed the boat, she'd never had the breaks, business had contracted, she'd never written a front page story, she hadn't changed the world. The closest she'd come to making a difference were a few freelance pieces for a broadsheet about the lack of facilities for disabled people at council swimming pools in East Kent – now she was settled into a routine of reporting for the local rag on missing dogs, unruly nightclubs and bad nursing homes. So when she woke up after her evening in Neptune's Hall and read the notes she'd made, she despaired. But it might be enough to keep her going. Local businessman's wife in love dash with toy-boy. Toy-boy gardener gives it to older woman in spades. Rakish behaviour at Hyde Hall. It might keep her bosses happy for a day or two, maybe longer. For sometimes these stories took on a life of their own and became more than the elaboration of local gossip, and grew arms and legs, and multiple heads.

When she told her editor she wanted to spend the morning investigating the story of a local butcher's wife who had gone off with the gardener, he laughed and told her to get over to Birchington where a tortoise was celebrating its one hundredth birthday. "And don't come back without some decent shots. In focus. And take the lens cap off."

"A tortoise? You're kidding."

"Oh my God!" he said. "Is that an intern waiting in reception? They'll be happy to work for nothing, you know for the…"

"Okay," she said. "I got it."

"Back here by three."

She drove slowly to Birchington, and her head played her dreams, and when she reached the house of the tortoise, and told the owner of the tortoise who she was, she was shown through to the garden to the shed of the tortoise, who was called Charles.

As soon as she saw the animal, Abigail knew something wasn't right, and as she interviewed the owner, she knew she was being fed lies. The question 'So how do you know Charles is one hundred years old?" was answered with averted eyes and a "Well, he was one when he was bought in Ramsgate by my grandfather."

"And when was that?"

"1915."

"But that would make him 98 years old."

"I mean… er… 1913. Yes. 1913. I think…"

"Okay." Abigail met people like this all the time, people so desperate to get their faces in the local paper that they'd do anything. She smiled and scribbled "Charles, 100, strolled his way to fame in a Birchington garden today, his ravaged shell displaying the scars and scuffs that have earned him the nickname 'Lucky'. Mrs Marjorie Swift, 76, of Sayer Avenue, explained that he was bought by her grandfather from a visiting Indian sailor, who had brought the plucky animal from his native country in a tea chest. 'He's always been a real part of the family, and still enjoys his lettuce and a stroll in the back garden.'"

When Abigail asked Mrs Swift if she could take a photograph of the ancient animal, she detected a certain reluctance, and it was only when she actually met the tortoise that she realised it was, in fact, dead. Its mummified head, tucked inside the dusty shell like an old man's cock, might have fooled some people, but Abigail knew. Not a lot got by her, and if it did, it was because she wanted it to. But now she was beginning to lose the will to do anything but nod and smile, so she said "Hold him up to your face so I can get a shot of the two of you together", and she took half a dozen shots before thanking Mrs Swift and getting out of the house before she had to accept the offer of a cup of tea and a stale biscuit.

On the way back to the office, Abigail allowed her mind to drift, and she thought about an old friend, a woman she hadn't seen for ten years. They'd had a falling out over a pair of boots, but she'd kept in touch with her career by reading her blog, her Twitter feed, and her regular pieces in *The Guardian*, *Frieze* and *Your Horse*. She'd have given the tortoise story some post-socialist spin, referenced Rex Mottram's gift to Julia Flyte, or turned it into an ironic critique of the fashion industry. This was the secret to success in this business – learn to take any subject and mould it to a mattress of ego and bullshit and self-promotion. Be ambition and knowledge, and your own seed.

What did Sartre say about choice? You take it, you sweep it, you cook it and have it. You collect it from your book and kneel on the floor and watch it twist. You give it the cash you've stolen, the money you've painted and the credit lost, and you wait. You wait, pack your bags and your vests, and you frame your nails. You meet, wait, push at a door and wash your bleeding hands. Abigail thought about these things as she climbed the stairs to the office, settled herself in her chair and started to write the story. The little words crept, and the pictures behind each letter ripped. And when she was done, she downloaded the photographs, chose one that made the tortoise look conscious, laid the piece out and winged it to her editor. Then she went to the coffee machine and watched as it made an Americano before going to stand on the fire escape to drink and smoke a cigarette and watch the car park. "Yeah," she said to no one at all, "whatever", and when she'd finished she flicked the butt at a passing seagull and went back to the office to check her emails. She read one from EVERY... magazine, a celebrity and real life gossip mag that used a network of stringers to fill their pages. From "Showbiz News" and "Hot Breaking" to "Sex and Your Relationships" and "Real Life Dramas", it dealt with the sort of bin juice that paid top bucks. She scanned the email and read: "We've just bought a piece about the *X Factor* contestant whose life was saved by Chicken Tikka, and as you probably know, the story of the girl from Dudley with the Jesus birthmark was syndicated in more than twenty countries. So if you're sitting on a tasty titbit you think we could run with, get in touch. We can only say 'No...'" She looked across the office. Through a gap in the blinds that shielded his office from view, she could see her editor, staring at his computer screen. "Yeah..." she whispered, and started to write an email. Subject: "Kent butcher's wife gives husband the chop. Gardener runs off with sizzling banger..." and outlined the story as told to her by Bert the gardener.

*

Fargo drove to Abergavenny station. A damp man in a uniform said he remembered a woman with a dog. She'd looked lost and lonely, and had caught an early train to Cardiff.

"You sure about that?"

"I should be."

"How did she look?"

The man shrugged. "I don't know. Like a woman?"

"Can I get a coffee?"

"Yes. Over there."

Fargo bought a coffee and went back to the car and drove on, and as his mind cleared and he put his foot down and hit the fast road to Newport, his thoughts swung from anger to some sort of understanding, over to not caring at all and back to anger. A yellow switch, a red kick and a purple bruise. A bunch of flowers, a sack of rocks, a dam across a swollen river. A yelled song, a cat on a roof, a wind. Because what was he doing with an old bird like Anne when he could be with a pretty girl his own age, her hair flying and her shining legs wrapped around his waist, her face pressed against his chest, her hand resting against the back of his neck, her red lips moving? Living the sort of life he wanted in a quiet corner of a small town, in a little flat over a bicycle shop with a view of the sea and steps down from the back garden to a garden where he could grow vegetables and soft fruit. Living without trouble or argument, without the threat of a mad husband or a fat dog, swinging through his days and into sweet, beating nights. But then – he thought – he'd have to watch as the pretty girl tired and then he'd have to listen as she complained that there was nothing to do and she wanted to go shopping in good shops with nice stuff not this crap, and she wanted to go to Ibiza and why aren't there any decent clubs round here and pass the vodka. Which was exactly why Anne was special. She wasn't interested in shopping or Spain or vodka, and she didn't care what colour her car was, and she didn't want to tell everyone what she'd just eaten and where she was going next. She liked to read old books and listen to old music and look at paintings in galleries, and when she wasn't doing any of those things she was happy to sit quietly and daydream, or tell him about a place she'd like to visit but never would. She was complicated but uncomplicated – did that make any sense? So it might not to anyone else but it did to him, and that was all he cared about.

And as he drove he thought about the other things he cared about, the small things – a good chicken sandwich with mayo, a windy beach with birds that did the darty thing birds do when the waves try and get them, red curtains, the way rear light clusters bend around the back of a car, the curve of a caravan roof, the twinkle of a bicycle wheel – and the big things. The big things were more difficult to pin down, but once he had one the rest followed. Ducks to a pond. So he cared about the world and that meant he cared about the sea and that meant he cared about the fact that there were too many fishermen in the world. And he cared about nurses. They weren't paid enough, and one day, when he was older and had more time, he was going to volunteer at a hospital. And he cared about fresh food, including proper sausages, vegetables in season and fruit that hadn't been ripened by gas in a big shed. And when he thought about sausages and how they should only be made from pork and seasoning and should never contain marmalade or pineapple or cheese, he thought about Anne and he saw that he had come full circle, and was pleased. Because whatever she thought about them and their relationship she was wrong. Whenever she had the idea that she too old or too fat or too slow for him, she was fooling herself. Maybe she had spent too long being told that she was all these things when she was none of them. Not one.

*

Harry Swaine woke late. He reached up. His head throbbed. He could feel his brain moving inside his skull, like it had grown legs and was trying to find a way out. Since the fiasco in Salisbury he'd been drinking without a break. Mainly canned lager, topped with whisky or rum. He'd reached a dead end. So Derek Muir and the men and women of UKTecs were still on the case, and even though he didn't have any faith in them, what else could he do? His wife and the boy could be anywhere. He had this idea that they'd gone to ground in somewhere like Birmingham or Manchester, a big place where you could disappear and never be found. But it was only an idea. Maybe they'd gone to Scotland.

He went downstairs and opened the fridge. He had a loaf of bread and some butter, and half a dozen lamb chops. He decided to have one for his breakfast. He found a frying pan and while he watched it cook, drank half a can of lager. As the drink went down he felt himself improve, so he flipped another chop into the pan and toasted some bread. Half an hour later, he saw Bert push a wheelbarrow past the kitchen window. The old man looked up and for a moment they stared into each others' eyes. Harry supposed he should go and say something. An apology was out of the question, but he might say something about the lawn looking good. A word of encouragement always went down well, even if it did stick in the throat. So when the chops were eaten, he fortified himself with another can of lager and went outside.

Bert was in his shed, sorting string. He was coiling lengths around his fingers and hanging them from hooks by the cobwebbed windows. At the sound of footsteps, he looked up and nodded. He mumbled "Morning…" but didn't stop what he was doing. He just carried on. He liked string. He could have talked about it all day.

"Just had a look at the back lawn," said Harry. "You've done a good job."

"Thank you, sir."

"And... yes, the greenhouse. The tomatoes. Good job with them too."

"I'll leave some by the back door."

Harry Swaine didn't eat cold vegetables unless he had to, but he took a deep breath and said "Thanks. And take what you want."

Bert nodded and Harry scratched the back of his head, and then he went back to the house to finish his beer. Half an hour later he was driving to Margate.

Whatever else happened in his life he had shops to watch, staff to stare at, sausages to check and plans to make. He wasn't sure what these plans would be but whatever – life went on, and even though he hated music, its notes had to follow one to another and another, and make some sort of tune.

*

And in the morning Margate offices of the *Thanet Express,* Abigail Grey twirled a pen and finished writing her email to EVERY... magazine. It asked a simple question. Would they be interested in a story about a butcher's wife who'd taken off with a gardener half her age? She sketched what she knew and said she knew it was a long shot, knew it was all a bit Connie and Mellors, but it was the silly season, life was short, and what the hell. It had all the ingredients, it was well seasoned, and it could run as long as its protagonists were running. Maybe longer. She clicked on 'send' and went to make a coffee, and when she got back to her computer a form reply was waiting for her. "Thanks for your interest in EVERY... magazine. We'll be in touch as soon as we can."

*

Cardiff station was grey and damp, and a fat wind blew down the platform, whipping litter onto the tracks and down the line towards the sidings and the weeds and broken signal boxes. The boxes and their hatted ghosts staring down at the points. Smashed windows and cracked wood. Stripped paint. Crows waiting. Corn dropped. Rotten steps and slipped tiles. A fox's den, a dumped fridge, a stack of rusting rails. Things wailing back into the earth, leaving a trace of the new or the recent but nothing else.

Anne had sat on a bench for an hour, watched two London trains come and go, and then gone to a café for a coffee. Music was playing. She loved music. She didn't care what it was – Mozart, the Rolling Stones, Tom Waits, Bach, Brahms, Joe Henry, Al Green, Count Basic, the Brighouse and Rastrick Band, Byrd, Biosphere, the Byrds. Harry Swaine hated music. He called it "pollution", just like "muck on the beach". So the music in the station café wasn't what she'd have chosen – generic British bubble rhythm – but it did set her thinking about the many things Harry hated. Public transport – "If they can't afford their own car they shouldn't be allowed to go anywhere." Organic food – "and giving a pig a bowl of muesli is going to make better bacon?" Doctors – "think they know everything just because they wear a white coat." Homosexualists – "don't get me started." Trees higher than fifteen feet – "bloody things stealing all the light." France – "think they're clever because they eat sparrows?" Marmalade – "call that breakfast?" The list went on and on, and the more it went on the more questions she asked herself. She understood why she'd married the man and understood why she'd stayed with him, but now – what was the point? If she thought she was safe with him, what was safety? And if she thought she could be happy with him, what was happiness? And if she thought he could give her security, did security mean anything? It meant nothing at all.

And then she thought about Fargo and his eyes and his mouth and how he was interested. And interesting. So maybe he wasn't interested in the things that interested her, but he was young and when you're young your ideas are never stuck. They float. One minute they're a boat, the next a car, then a motorbike. Or a pair of boots. Fargo had a pair of black boots. She didn't know what brand they were, or even if they were a brand, but they suited him. And maybe suiting things was the key. Or a key. And do keys have to have locks? Or locks doors? Too many questions.

Fargo climbed the steps to the platform and saw Anne sitting on the bench. She was sitting with a straight back. Radar was lying down, his chin resting in the cross of his paws. She knew he was coming but didn't look up. She'd been waiting and thinking about the things she was going to say, but as the seconds collapsed she gave up and let it go. And when he was standing next to her, she took a deep breath and filled her lungs with his smell. The smell of a new road. The taste of a new road she'd never travelled, filling her up. And she heard something, a bird singing from its perch on the rusted beams of the platform's canopy, a metaphor if you will, some Spanish castle magic or an axis that would never shift. He said her name and she looked up. There were tears in her eyes. She reached up to wipe them as he reached down to wipe them, and their fingers touched. "I'm sorry…" she said. "I never thought… and…"

"Don't say anything else," he said. "Please?"

"Okay."

"I've got the car."

"Good."

*

The road from Cardiff was busy but didn't feel like it. Like a hexagram of its own trip, it cast itself blind and scrambled its way to Newport and Abergavenny and the Black Mountain. And as the country opened its arms so the miles rolled, and the views became their music. And Anne chose some music, and she watched the side of Fargo's face take the morning light, and his hair, and she listened as Radar snored a light rumble on the back seat. And when they stopped at a roadside café and sat to drink coffee, she closed her eyes and listened to the swish of the traffic.

They'd talked. They'd said:

"You came back."

"Of course I did."

"But when I woke up this morning, I looked at you... I looked at you and I thought..."

"What did you think?"

"I thought... I can't wreck your life."

"How could you wreck my life?"

"I'm old enough to be your mother."

"What's that got to do with it?"

"You should be with someone your own age."

"No I shouldn't. I should be with you."

"Why?"

"Because someone my own age would be an idiot."

"They're not all idiots."

"No. But the ones I've met have been, and now I've found you I know."

"You know what?"

"That the rest don't matter. I want you, Anne. You teach me."

"I teach you?"

"Yes."

"I don't know anything."

"You don't need to."

"But..."

"But nothing," said Fargo, and the words rested in the air between them and twisted and then sank, and like a feather settled in the nest.

*

It was a busy morning at the *Thanet Express*. A big story was breaking. Abigail's editor had had a call from the local plod, and it was a good one. Plenty of detail, lashings of blood, a seasoning of sex. The evening before, as the sun had sunk into a bank of fat grey clouds, a man from Ramsgate had come home from work in his Canterbury office. Earlier in the day, he'd called his wife to say he'd be late, but at 5:30 he'd changed his mind and decided that the week had been tough enough, and all he wanted to do was slump in front of the TV with a beer and a pizza. So when he let himself in the back door and saw his wife bent over the kitchen table while their neighbour gave her a vigorous work-out with a range of rechargeable tools, he quickly shifted from tired to unhinged, grabbed the first thing he saw – an umbrella – and stuck the neighbour in his eye. Pierced to the brain, the man had died, but not before the wife had battered the husband to a pulp with a kettle while screaming 'What did you expect? He had a ladder!" Now, with one man in the morgue, another in intensive care, a woman in custody and two children in the care of the local authority, Abigail Grey felt overwhelmed. So when she got an email from EVERY... magazine to say that they were interested in her story about the butcher and his wife, she had a brief meltdown. They explained that if she gave them the inside track they'd put the story out to their hounds, and their hounds were hungry. Depending on the outcome, she could be looking at £5,000 minimum, and if it was a roll-over, plenty more. She replied with a quick one – "Let me get back to you pm – breaking story here I've got to deal with..." and went to see her editor.

He gave her the up-down fuckery on the cuckold/murder story. "His name's Derek Muir. Private detective, home address, 25 Rendell Avenue, Ramsgate. Works in Canterbury for a company called UKTecs. Get over to the house, take some shots, talk to the neighbours, then check out his office. Third floor, 145 Lincoln Street. Don't suppose you'll have any joy but see what you can do."

She did exactly what she could do, managed to get a quote from a neighbour – "They were such a lovely family. It's not the sort of thing you expect round here..." and another from the woman who ran a corner shop – "The kids used to come in all the time. I can't believe it..." She took some shots of the house, the police tape that straddled the drive, and a long shot of the road. Then she drove over to Canterbury, rang the buzzer next to the UKTecs sign, and when a woman's voice answered, introduced herself. She got a curt "No comment..." so she crossed to the other side of the road, walked to a place where the cathedral was in shot, and took a picture of the office building. Then she went to a café and had a cup of coffee.

As she drank, she made some notes, clicked through the photos she'd taken, trawled her phone, listened to a couple of messages and then pulled a book from her bag and read for twenty minutes. She always had a book on the go, and as long as it didn't have any pink on the cover or featured a character called Miranda, she read anything. Today she was working her way through the diaries of Samuel Pepys. Every new year she promised herself that she'd write a diary, an insightful and honest account of her life, her work and her search for love, but she'd never got further than half way through February without giving up. Or forgetting. Or doing whatever it is that people do when they stop writing something.

She adored Samuel Pepys and his honesty, his fun and his angry wife. One day she would write her diary and it would be as true as a field. For how many diarists could you trust, and how many treated themselves as proper, faulted subjects? He and Mrs Knipp had just managed to escape some robbers. "Oh Mr Pepys!" cried Mrs Knipp, and her laughing voice bounced down the years like a rubber ball on cobbles, and met her at a door.

*

Fargo, Anne and Radar headed down a road that looked familiar but wasn't. It was grey and tall. The stretches were blown with spray and filth but the car was warm and runny and musty, and rank with the smell of damp dog. That smell that might remind you of the smell you get when you open a cheese lover's fridge. Rich, sweet, not long for this world. Take it. Breathe. All the saturated fat you could eat, some hard and some soft, and some open. Fetch some biscuits. Sit down. Put your feet up. Eat. Have a stroke. Go to hospital. Lie in a bed. Blame someone else. Recover. Go home. Have some more cheese.

Fargo and Anne were calm. After their hiatus something had cleared and they were comfortable to sit together and let the landscape come, leave, repeat and remind. A castle and a flag. What did the flag mean? What did any flag mean? Hills and mountains, rivers, steep fields, slate walls, sheep. If they had things to flag or say these things could wait. Put them in a cupboard and let them sweat and get used to the dark. And if they didn't have things to say, maybe that was better. Sometimes Anne wondered if people talked too much, were just too happy to express themselves. Words could be a pollution, like the world was the sea and words were the scraps of plastic that kill turtles. And that was without the clamour of books, the endless pity of those pages, hundreds and thousands and millions of rustling pages, all crinkled and getting in everyone's ears. But silence wasn't a disease, it didn't have to be uncomfortable, or the bandage on something that was. So when, after they'd been driving for a couple of hours, and Fargo indicated and pulled into the car park of a roadside café, Anne said nothing and he said nothing. And as they climbed out of the car they were quiet, and only Radar said something, a single gruff bark as he lumbered towards a lamp post.

The café was a time warp – red vinyl banquettes, Formica topped tables, glass sugar shakers, framed posters of Elvis posing on scaffolding, black and white tiles on the floor and a bowl of plastic flowers on the counter. When they walked in, Billy Fury was playing, and then Buddy Holly. They ordered coffee and sat at a window table, and while Fargo drew a smiley face in the window's condensation, Anne scanned the menu and thought about having something to eat. Maybe an omelette. She liked omelettes, and hadn't eaten one for ages.

"I'm hungry," she said. These were the first words she'd spoken for over an hour. "I think I'll have an omelette." She closed the menu, put it on the table, laid her hand on it and smiled at Fargo. She didn't wonder any more. Doubt had cleared from her mind, and if there was danger around the corner she didn't care. It meant nothing. All she cared about was the road ahead, and maybe an omelette.

"An omelette?" said Fargo.

"Yes."

"I haven't had an omelette for ages."

"Nor have I."

"I might have one too," he said, and picked up the menu and read it and said "Cheese and mushroom?"

"Cheese," said Anne, and as the word came out she felt it roll across her lips like a special tongue, and after the waitress had taken their order, she sat back and closed her eyes and let Fargo hold her hand across the sticky table.

*

Harry sat in the office of his Margate shop, ate a sausage roll, drank a can of beer and decided he needed cheering up. He deserved a sideboard of bottles and a woman. Maybe a pair of women. And some decent tunes, a few smokes and low lights. So when he'd finished eating, he opened another can, took out his phone and made a call.

"Reflections."

"Hey Maureen."

"Who's this?"

"Harry."

"Harry?"

"Yeah. Who's on?"

"Rosie, Olga and Stevie."

"What about tomorrow?"

"The same. And Bobbie."

"The big one?"

"You know she is, Harry."

He took a breath. "Okay. Bobbie and Rosie..."

"Okay."

"They're free to party at mine?"

"At yours?"

"Yeah, problem with that?"

"It's just... You're usually..."

"I know what I usually do."

"Whatever, Harry. You pay, they party."

"I'll send a cab. Half nine?"

"You know the form."

"Mo..."

"Cash in hand."

"Oh please," he said, and he hung up, tossed the paper on the desk and closed his eyes. He watched the back of his lids and for half a minute saw nothing but dots of light in the fields of darkness, black and yellow, flashes there, slashes coming, a toss and a galaxy against the flight of rage. A vision, maybe, or was it simply a trip that happened when you closed your eyes? Sometimes he wondered about god, or should he think this thing was clouds? Earth? Pork chops? The perfect, raging sun? A swelling tit against the clot of his life? Bacon? Harry Swaine? Dust of stars? Can it ever be so, so shown in happiness or failure, or in the colours of the twisting toss of what we take? Everyone sometimes changes, he thought, and then his thoughts failed, and he laid his head down, and he slept.

*

The machines that monitored Derek Muir beeped, the air around his bed crackled, and a policeman sat in the corridor beyond the sterile area. This man didn't know why he was there or how long he would have to stay but there he was and there he would be and he could spend an hour picking lint off his trousers. Muir had killed his wife's lover but he wasn't going anywhere soon. So the policeman was bored but as least he had nurses to look at. Some of them made him want to sob. With their scrubs and their aprons and their hair tied up, they were visions to him, and when he got tired of thinking how they might be, he could always try to recall the name of every football league ground in the UK.

Derek's brain twinkled with shards of bone, his skull was swathed in wraps of bandage, and his ventilator and nasogastric tube quivered with labour. Every few minutes a nurse would come and check his comfort, adjust a valve or a pump setting, go back to her station and make a mark in his notes. The people who worked on the unit lived heightened lives, long periods of tedium punctuated by moments of extreme and vital activity. The guardians of the last tunnels, they were also technicians of the cusp between death and the whistled notes of the unlikely. So when one of Derek's machines gave out a single buzz and triggered a red light at the station, the nurse pushed a call button and rushed to the patient.

He was convulsing, little flecks of spittle spotted his cheeks and his fingers were quivering. A moment later his back arched, he gave out an echoed sigh, went into spasm, the monitors flashed and as the nurse calmly checked the saline, a doctor came, took one look and said "Stroke".

"Do I..."

"We need to..." but before he could finish the sentence, Derek relaxed, dropped back onto the bed and wheezed. His mouth gaped and his eyes opened for the first time since he'd taken the blow from his wife, and the nurse saw an understanding there, and a resignation. And after a minute of thought and memory, an ordered recall of all the good things he'd enjoyed in his half-done life, he died. His end was that quick and didn't come as a shock to anyone, and after a moment of silence, the doctor put his hand on the nurse's shoulder, gave it a squeeze and left. She waited another moment, listened to the doctor's footsteps as they faded down the corridor, then closed his eyes and started to unplug the body.

Ten miles away, Abigail had received another email from EVERY... magazine. They were keen on her story and their stringers were ready to go to work and was she going to forward details? They underlined and reiterated their terms and the benefits that could be heading her way. These – they repeated – involved a minimum of £5,000 and possibly more. Yeah, she thought, and she thought about how it was time she bought a week of shopping in New York City, so she sketched what she knew of the story, found a library shot of Anne and Harry Swaine, a couple of archived stories about the man's chain of shops, sent the lot out and went to finish a story about the installation of automatic floodlights at a controversial skateboard park in Broadstairs.

*

Fargo's omelette was good and packed with ham, Anne's omelette was filled with cheese and mushrooms, the dash from the restaurant to the car was swift, and as they left the Black Mountains and drove further in the country, the rain settled in for the afternoon, the views deepened and they stopped talking about the past. They would never look over the shoulders and consider the poverty of mistake. They would only think and talk about the future, and they would make mottos from its promise.

She said "The is is the was of what will be."

"Eh?"

"I read it somewhere."

"You're going to tell me what books I should read," he said.

"Am I?"

"You can try," he said, and then he told her that when he was a kid he didn't have much time for reading because he spent all his spare time making plans for his bike shop.

"Your bike shop?"

"It was a dream I had."

"Dreams are good."

"Yeah. I used to spend all my time on my bike. Soon as I got in from school I was on it. Used to meet up with my mate and ride all over the place. And when I couldn't go out, if it was wet or something, I used to spend hours just cleaning it, polishing the handlebars with this chrome cleaning stuff I found, fiddling with the gears and brakes, getting it just right. One day it just seemed so obvious – when I was old enough and I'd saved enough, I'd open my own shop. I still think it's a good idea. People love their bikes, and they always need servicing from someone who knows what they're doing."

"They do. And you think you'd make a good bike shop owner?"

"Why not? I still make plans for it…"

"Go on…"

"I'd have the workshop out the back and a place in the front where the customers could wait and have a cup of coffee and a piece of cake."

"Okay. Want me to bake the cakes?"

"That's what I was hoping you'd say. It'll be the first bike and cake shop in the country."

"That's such a good plan."

"People would come for miles," he said, and he told her that if they found a big enough place they could do more than tea and cakes, and offer meals, packed lunches and home made smoothies. And then maybe even beds for the night, a camping barn, a hostel, a full service. And as he talked she smiled and nodded and thanked him for showing her something she thought she'd never see again. A plan, a purpose, a window. And when they reached Rhayader, the road followed the course of a full river and more windows opened, the rain eased and blue sky appeared in the west.

Some time in the afternoon, they turned west and followed the signs to Aberystwyth. The road steamed as it dried, and as more sunlight broke through the clouds, so the fields and hedges and trees sang with birds.

*

In the offices of EVERY... magazine, the air crackled and spat, and the workers lived in a state of constant half-panic. The office bully planned her next move, an intern checked her phone, a writer thought about having a minor heart attack. Phones rang, plants wilted, earphones hissed, and celebrity news played on a row of screens. The place smelled of fish and sweat and plastic. In a corner office, the boss leant back in her chair and chewed a pen. She got through three a day. Always red, always cheap. One of her project managers sat opposite, and stared at his shoes. Nervous, flooded with testosterone and running with sweat, he was at a constant loss. He dreamed as he half-listened as she talked about the story Abigail had sent over. It had been a slow week, so she was happy to have something they could chase, even though it might not have legs.

"But even if it hasn't, we'll make some, won't we Tony?"

He snapped back to reality. "Some what?"

"Legs."

"Okay."

"So do we have any idea where they are?"

"Last seen in Salisbury."

"Where?"

"Wiltshire? Hampshire? Somewhere like that."

"Cow land?"

"Yeah. Cow land."

"And when was that?"

"A couple of days ago. And our woman thinks they'll be heading west or north."

"And why does she think that?"

"The husband lives in the south east."

"Figures. Okay."

"And we've got pictures?"

"Yeah, of her. None of him, but a good description. And we know what sort of car they're in, and they've got a dog with them. Once the word's out, I give it a day or two."

"Cool."

"So I'll brief the troops."

"You brief the troops…"

Half an hour later, an email was dropping into the inbox of stringers from Penzance to Cardiff, and from Chester to Aberdeen. The usual terms, the standard rates, and the sharper the pics the better. "Lately we've been getting some pretty ropey shots, so pull your fingers out, guys. If you can't figure out how to use auto-focus, ask a policeman."

*

That evening, Anne, Fargo and Radar arrived in Aberystwyth, checked into a tall hotel, took a room with a view of the promenade, the beach and the bay, congratulated themselves and went for a drink. It was a beautiful evening. The rain had stopped and as the sun set it layered the sky with stripes and clots of orange, yellow and red. They found a bar with a terrace and as they sat and drank and picked at a bowl of nuts, happy families played on the sand, wind surfers skimmed the waves and couples strolled arm in arm.

Anne had a gin and tonic, Fargo had a pint of lager and as they drank they held hands. She was wearing a little silver ring on her little finger – he twisted it and for a moment thought about asking where she'd got it, but he didn't. Lovers should have secrets, he thought. They shouldn't have to tell each other everything. A hidden place is a good place.

"I've had another idea," he said.

"Another?"

"Yeah. I'm full of them."

"I know…"

"We open a snack bar."

"A snack bar?"

"Yeah. Except it sells really good food. No rubbish burgers and instant coffee. It'll be a gourmet snack bar."

"Well, good luck with that."

"Don't you think it's a good idea?"

"People who eat at snack bars want a rubbish burger and instant coffee. They don't want line-caught salmon with chervil and kumquat pesto…"

"They might. You'll never know until you try it…"

"Fargo?" She squeezed his hand and then leant towards him and kissed his cheek.

"What?"

"If you think you're going sell that sort of stuff to a hungry lorry driver from Huddersfield, you need to think again. Stick with the bike shop idea. Bikes and cakes. That makes a lot more sense."

"Okay," he said, but he didn't let the gourmet snack bar idea go. He filed it away and went back to his pint, stroked Radar's head and stared at the view.

A couple of hours later, and after some plates of pasta in the hotel restaurant, they walked along the promenade and through the town until they reached the marina, and strolled around, looking at the yachts and fishing boats.

"Want to hear a story?" he said.

"Go on then."

"The other week. The night before your old man and I had that fight. Remember?"

"How could I forget?"

"That night before, I stole a boat from Broadstairs harbour."

"You what?"

"I was drunk. I rowed around for a bit and then the sea got rough… I ended up crashing it onto the beach at Louisa Bay."

"You didn't."

"That's why I had that bruise."

She shook her head. "Crazy boy…"

"I don't know what got into me." He pointed to a little rowing boat attached to the side of a yacht. "It was like that one."

"But that's tiny."

"I know."

"Crazy…"

"Tell me about it…"

They walked along a bit further. Radar thought about chasing a seagull. She said "Promise me something."

"What?"

"You won't do anything like that again."

"I promise."

"Cross your heart?"

'Already done."

*

Harry Swaine, butcher, control freak, fat, and with less self-awareness than a bag of gravel, sat in his favourite chair and stared at a bottle of Baileys. He'd bought it for his party, but when he thought about the word 'party' his head went into a spin because he wasn't really having a party. Not a proper one. At least he didn't think it was. The last real party he'd been to had been a couple of years before in Ramsgate. Something arranged by the Association of Thanet Butchers. It had been held in the bar of a winter hotel, and had descended into chaos when someone from a shop in Whitstable had tried to gatecrash the gathering.

"Whitstable?"

"Yeah. And?"

"That's not Thanct."

"So?"

Bosh.

Harry remembered. There'd been dozens of people there and crisps, nuts and sausage rolls to eat. No. This was going to be a party. This was going to be a thing. So should he buy crisps and nuts, or sausage rolls for his thing? He didn't want to sound like a idiot by phoning Maureen and asking her what Bobbie and Rosie liked to eat, but he did think about it. But then he didn't. He didn't like to think too much.

He stared at the bottle of Baileys and he stared at a bottle of Bell's, and he stared at a bottle of gin. Women drank gin. They liked gin. They loved gin. They loved those botanicals. Of course they did. Gin and tonic, ice and a slice, tall glass, lots of bubbles up your nose, lovely. He got up, poured himself a slug of Bell's, lit a cigarette, took a deep drag and thought about music. Music to get up and dance to. Tunes. So tunes were pollution but women loved them so he'd listen and he'd watch.

He went to the rack of CDs in the corner of the room and ran his fingers down them until he found Get That Party Started Vol 2. All the best tunes were there – Cyndi Lauper and her Girls Just Wanna Have Fun, The Weather Girls and Raining Men, Sheena Easton's Morning Train, Belinda Carlisle singing Heaven

Is A Place On Earth. A god-awful selection of nonsense, the sort of stuff you might want to hide from, but it would get them in a sophisticated mood and fill the room with promise. He tossed the CD onto a coffee table and sat down again, and carried on staring at the bottles. And as he stared, something stirred in his chest, something he didn't recognise. He tried to work out what it was but couldn't. So he sipped his drink and closed his eyes and as his stomach burned, he remembered.

He remembered a family holiday, and he recalled feelings of pleasure and happiness. They'd stayed on a caravan site outside Weymouth, a place with a sandy beach and good pubs. Mike and Robert had been, what? Eight and six? Buckets and spades and ice cream and grazed knees. And he remembered they found a restaurant where they could sit with a view of the harbour and watch the fishing boats come and go. And he remembered – though he could hardly think straight when he did – how Anne had been happy and one evening, after the boys had gone to bed, they'd sat in deckchairs and drunk wine and watched the sun set and talked about how maybe they could move to this beautiful place.

Holiday talk.

Holiday happiness.

He opened his eyes.

He closed them again.

*

The morning broke clear and blue over the moon of Aberystwyth's beach. It was the first clear day of the month, the first day for weeks that hadn't threatened rain. The air smelt of salt and liquorice and iodine. Swifts, surprised by the sky, darted from their places, and a hawk watched their flight. The numbers climbed, workers crawled, lovers rolled towards each other, the sun rose, a road steamed.

Anne woke first, got out of bed, went to the window, opened the curtains and looked out. As Fargo slept on he made small noises, like a mouse in a hole. She went back to bed, leant towards him and touched his nose, and ran her fingers over his forehead. She reached down and stroked his chest, moved down to his belly button and made circles around it. His eyes flicked and he sniffed. One eye opened. Them the other. She felt that one twitch against the back of her hand and he rolled towards her, flopped an arm over and pinched her waist. She loved his touch and the feel of his fingers, and the play of light on the bed.

They ordered breakfast in their room. Toast, orange juice, tea, scrambled eggs, some bacon, mushrooms. When it arrived, they sat up to eat at a table by the window, watched the morning walkers, the rolling waves and the sky. A bus, a few cars, another bus. A man on his bicycle, steering with one hand. A cat passed by in a flash, and a lady in a bright orange dress. A trailer, another bus. A dog barked and pigeons flew up and fluttered around. An early policeman and three men crawling on their way to work. "Why?" said Fargo.

"Why what? said Anne.

"I've no idea," said Fargo.

But breakfast was, they both agreed, the most delicious they'd ever eaten, and later, as they strolled along the beach and threw a stick for Radar and watched him jump through the waves, he said "This place reminds me of Margate, but without the Margate bits."

She laughed. "I wonder if it needs a bike shop."

"You can never have too many bike shops, Miss Carter."

"Is that true?"

"It might be."

They reached the end of the promenade and the ticket office of the railway that climbed Constitution Hill. A train was pulling into the station, so they bought tickets and climbed aboard.

The trip was slow and odd and refreshing, and when they reached the top they headed towards the café for a cup of coffee and half an hour with the view. The bay was the deepest blue, and cut with the wakes of half a dozen little boats, some fishing, others drifting, two anchored, none stolen. In the far distance, a pair of white sails, above a flight of puffy clouds. Between the clouds, the trail of a high plane, heading west. Around them, other people were enjoying the morning, and when they stood up and Radar pulled them towards the coast path, Anne took Fargo's arm and said "I could live here".

"Me too."

"It's so beautiful."

"It's like a postcard."

"But…"

"But what?" They had walked away from the crowds, from the eyes and ears, and the noses.

She shook her head.

"You wobbling again?"

"No, Fargo. I'm not wobbling."

"Good…"

"But if we're going to do this, really do it, we have to be practical. We'll run out of money before you know it, and we can't live on air…"

"I know," he said, "so I'll pick up the local newspaper and look for a job…"

"You'll do that?"

"Of course. I'm not stupid. I know the score. I know what we have to do…" and as these words came out of his mouth and settled in her ears, she felt something new. Maybe it was a future or maybe it was just a plan, or maybe his words were just sounds, but when they reached a place where it seemed right to turn around and walk back, they did without suggestion, as if they were one person and a single dog beneath the deep blue sky.

*

Back at the café on the hill, a man with a camera drank a cup of tea, thought about having a cake and waited. Ray Craske had seen them on the promenade, taken a dozen shots and noted this: they weren't trying to hide or disguise who they were. They looked like they were enjoying a pleasant holiday, which – Ray supposed – they were. He'd trailed them down the promenade, stopped as they spent half an hour throwing a stick for the dog, took some more shots then followed them to the railway, watched them take a train to the top, waited for the next, took that and saw them again drinking coffee at a café table, laughing, stroking the dog, pointing at the boats in the bay. When they stood up and headed off down the coast path he thought about following them, but knew they wouldn't go far. He was right. Half an hour later they were back, and when they took the train back to town, he joined them, and sat a few rows behind them, wiped the sweat from his face with a grey handkerchief, and listened.

The train rattled and shook so he only heard snatched words – "Hotel..." "Caravans..." "Lunch..." 'The car...' – and when they reached the bottom they headed back along the promenade. Once again Ray followed at a discrete distance, and took a few shots as they walked arm in arm and laughed at the dog. Before they reached the pier, they crossed the road and stepped into a hotel. He took a shot of the place, then turned away, walked to the

Inn on the Pier, ordered a pint, took a table with a good view of the promenade, and started to scroll through the camera.

He'd done well. Fifty-two shots, and at least half of them in focus. He took out his notebook and sketched out the last few hours – spotting them on the promenade, trailing them up Constitution Hill and back the way they'd come and on to the hotel – and made a few random notes about how they appeared carefree and oblivious to the storm that was swirling in their wake, and then he settled back to enjoy his pint.

*

At Hyde Hall, the preparations were almost complete. There were no decorations but the bottles stood in their groups, glasses shone, the CD player blinked, the fridge hummed and nuts were piled in glass bowls. Harry sat in his favourite chair and called Reflections to confirm the time. Half nine it was. No problem. Bobbie and Rosie. Nice. Yes. He wanted them to do an all-nighter. And yes. He'd pay cash. Up front. What else did they expect? Christ descending in a Peugeot?

At half five the back door bell rang. It was Bert. He was holding his bicycle. Some onions and beans were piled in its basket. He looked at Harry and wondered why the man was wearing jeans and the sort of shirt footballers wore when they were interviewed after a match. It had a wide collar and was unbuttoned to the middle of his chest. And the man had grease on his hair and smelt like a chemist's shop. It was all Bert could do not to say something but he bit his lip and looked at the ground when he said "I'm off home. See you in the morning."

"No," said Harry. "I won't need you tomorrow. Take the day off."

"You sure about that? The lawns need edging."

"They can keep."

"And I was going to do some greenhouse work. The tomatoes need spraying."

"They can keep too."

"But…"

"They'll keep, Bert."

"I really should do something about…"

"Take the day off, Bert! Have it on me, okay?"

"Oh. Right." Bert could see there was no point arguing. Best go. "See you on Friday."

"You will," said Harry, and he closed the door.

Bert turned and climbed onto his bicycle and pedalled away, and when he reached the bottom of the drive, took the road into down and stopped at Neptune's Hall for a pint. As he ordered, he looked around, half hoping that he'd see the woman he'd met, the one who took such an interest in his life, but she wasn't there, so he found a chair in the corner, and sat to drink and think about lawns and greenhouse vegetables and/or fruit.

*

Eighty miles away, another man stared into a glass, waited for a moment and finished his drink. Then Robert Swaine, eldest son of Harry and Anne Swaine of Hyde Hall, Kent, waited, thought about his evening, poured another and squinted. The drink was the colour of amber. He looked at it and swilled it and listened to the chink of the ice and then he watched the river. It was sluggish. Pale. Grey. The river was not the thing it should have been. The river was a drain.

Plastic bottles, plastic bags, a traffic cone, lumps of wood. The slop of the city. All its sins and guilt and shame and pain. The week before, a body had nudged the wall below his flat. Fat and bloated and rank, it had attracted gulls and sirens, and a police launch. A helicopter in the sky, its flight meeting the launch's light, his own lights paling and poor. Voices raised, orders given, orders obeyed, and he'd wondered what it would be like to be a policeman. All that filth and grief and abuse and for what? A month's salary equivalent to his day rate. Was there more? He didn't know.

Now a pleasure boat headed downstream, carrying tourists to Greenwich, the witch and the museum. What would they do when they got there? Wander and shop, stop and stare, wonder why they were there? Would they enjoy their day, or be bored and despair and get tired. Robert was tired. Tired of work, of colleagues, numbers, air conditioning, a full inbox and filth. He wanted to get out of the city. He had to get out of the city. He had to do something spontaneous and quick. He had to surprise himself. What was the thing someone had said to him in the pub? "Scare yourself every day, Rob. It's what I do."

He picked up his glass carried it to the sink, tossed the drink and the ice and went to his bedroom. He pulled a case out of the wardrobe and stuffed it with some clothes and a wash bag, grabbed a jacket and ten minutes later he was sitting in traffic on the Old Kent Road. The office could go to hell. The stakeholders could hang. The city could fail and the lights die, and what could they do to him? He could go anywhere he wanted.

*

And then Ray finished writing the brief but arresting story of Anne, Fargo and Radar's life in Aberystwyth. He'd let the people at EVERY... magazine add their own spin to the copy, but he gave them all the information he knew they'd want, the rough lies, the usual, the things he'd been taught, the stuff about how Fargo was tousled and moody and fit, and sometimes looked like the woman had kidnapped him and he was trapped, unable to get away even if he wanted to. And then he wrote that both of them seemed to spend most of the time drunk because although these photos were taken between half ten and midday, what you couldn't see was the bottle of vodka she was swigging from. And then he added that the dog looked ready and dangerous and fierce. And he added that people at the hotel had heard them talking in the middle of the night, and then the talking had turned to a different type of noise. And then he chose a dozen of the best, sharpest pictures, attached them to the email and pinged it. He watched it disappear and then half an hour later he was in his local for a celebratory drink, a laugh with the barman and a look at the three women who sat at a table by the door, their hair so long and their legs glistening like the pins in some god's sewing basket.

*

The cab turned, passed through the gates and rumbled up the drive to Hyde Hall. The headlights illuminated the trees and shrubs and borders. Birds burst, cats popped and ran, gravel spat, mice failed. Bobbie and Rosie adjusted their tops, smoothed their skirts and checked their breath. They checked their breath and then they checked their teeth. Their teeth were good. The driver looked in the mirror, licked his lips and stopped by the front door. He was tired and wanted to go home. A light clicked on, a latch flicked, the door opened and Harry stepped out. He gave the driver a twenty, said "Hello…" to the women and watched their moves as they stepped inside. They were wearing short summer jackets. He followed them in, closed the door, and led the way down the hall to the sitting room. They dropped their bags on the sofa and he said "Fancy a drink?"

Bobbie sucked air and said "Do I?"

"I don't know. Do you?"

She looked at the row of bottles, looked at Rosie, looked back at the bottles and said "Vodka and tonic?"

"Sure," he said, "And you're..."

"Rosie..."

"Rosie."

"The same, ta."

As he fixed the drinks, the women checked the room. There were pictures on the wall – one of a New York City skyline, another of waves breaking around a lighthouse, another of a fishing boat pulled up on a tropical beach. Two sofas at right angles to each other, a large television, a low table, low lights and some ornaments and knick-knacks on painted shelves. A CD player blinked and Chris de Burgh whined.

"So," said Harry. He felt odd. He tried to identify the feeling which was tight and rooted in his chest. Was he nervous? Tense? He wasn't sure. Bobbie wasn't, and nor was Rosie. They didn't care. "Have a seat," he said. "Don't be shy."

"Oh, we're never shy, are we Rosie?"

"Never."

"Wouldn't do, not in our line of work."

"No, it wouldn't."

They sat together on one of the sofas, drank and Bobbie said "Mind if we smoke?"

"Be my guest," said Harry. And he fetched an ashtray. As he put it on the table, Rosie said "Let's get the business out of the way..."

"Sure." He pulled a roll of notes out of his pocket and handed it over. "Six hundred."

"Good man," and she started to count it.

"You don't need to do that."

"Habit, love. And a good one."

Half an hour later, he was following them up the stairs and down the corridor to the bedroom, watching them as they twitched and shimmied, and then he was telling them that this was the bed and this is what I want you to do and what I want you to do is what you want to do but you'd better do it like you mean it, and then, while they went to the en-suite and did what they had to do, he kicked his shoes off, unbuckled his belt, dropped his trousers, tossed them to one side and sat in a chair by the window with his socks and shirt on. He poured a drink and listened to the sound of water running and quiet whispering. Then the bathroom door opened and the women appeared.

He was happy with what he saw. They wobbled and spilled and shone, and gave off the smell of the block, knives and bins of his shops. They walked towards him but he put a hand up and said "On the bed, girls, and do what comes naturally. Or unnaturally. Your choice. I'll be over here."

"Okay," said Bobbie. "You're the boss."

"You noticed."

"Oh yeah."

So the women moved towards the bed, and Rosie lay back and hauled herself towards the pillows and Bobbie followed her, crawling and cupped, and the music skipped to something else, a song he didn't recognise. But he didn't care and they didn't care, and as the women worked the light in the room seemed to dim, as if it could see and didn't want to see. And there was a change in the temperature too. The warmth was cut and although Harry tried to focus, he couldn't. He sat and for the first time in his life, he felt pointless. Pointless and hopeless and some other less that he couldn't define, and even another drink failed him.

*

The road shone and the lights cast their skint light, and Robert Swaine steered his car south and then east. The radio played something he didn't recognise, a cigarette fumed, the windscreen wipers swept and cleaned, swept and cleaned, swept and cleaned. He had emptied his mind so nothing troubled him – no thoughts about work or neighbours or the river and family or friends. Emptiness. This is what he craved. A new start, a clean slate, a ditch he could lie in and from where he could watch the stars and listen to the night crawlers. It could be a wet ditch or it could be a dry one but it had to be a peaceful one.

He recalled something, his earliest memory, he supposed. His mother had gone to have a hair cut and had left him in the corner of the shop. He remembered the smell of the hair and the shampoo and how the hairdressers and other customers had cooed over him, and he'd entertained them by laughing and singing along with songs on the radio. And then he'd grown tired and had fallen asleep, and when he woke up his mother had gone. The first abandonment, he thought. The first – and maybe the last, he wasn't sure about this – time that he'd ever felt terror. A feeling he used as an ingredient in the recipe he would eventually use to build himself a carapace.

And the road shone on and Robert drove on, and he began to feel sleepy so he opened the window and flicked the cigarette and let the rain and air chill his face, and a tune he recognised came on the radio, something with a lyric about how if you spend too long in one place you begin to feel old. He got that.

And the night was black and orange and cut, and the car was fast, and even though he felt sleepy he felt alive so he pushed the car some more, and when he reached a place where he could move to the outside lane, he put his foot down and pulled away like he'd been shot, and the spray rose and the engine whined and spun, and everything he wished became a sort of light in his ears, or a smell at his fingertips, or the laziness of a man who knows exactly what he can do, and does it.

The A2 leaked into the M2 and the night darkened and Robert found more space and more speed, and he tipped his head back and held the wheel with one faint hand, and everything was so good. The rain and the black and the glow of the dashboard lights, and more music, such beautiful music. A woman's voice and then a man's, and a low saxophone playing like a valley. Who said you should never take a saxophone seriously? Whoever it was needed to be taken to the bank and pushed.

And the motorway rolled on, it rolled like a perfect hit, the one he took in a city bar with a woman whose name he just could not remember but it did begin with the letter J, and he remembered how her fingers just would not stop wrapping around his, like they were some sort of bird's fingers, if birds had fingers.

*

And forty miles away, Harry's women raised their game but the pointlessness had become futility and the feelings he'd been expecting had failed and been replaced by a nagging and a pulling, something malevolent and heavy, and pushy. And then a prickly sensation flooded his legs, his arms and his face. He closed his eyes and heard bells and saw lights and he moaned, and when he opened them again the women were staring at him, all pretence forgotten, their arms crossed and their mouths open as though they were virgins surprised.

"You okay, Harry?" said Bobbie.

He nodded.

"You don't look so good."

"I'm…" he said. "I think I'm…"

"Oh bollocks," said Rosie, and she slid off the bed and went to him and took his hand. "He's having a heart attack."

"Jesus…"

"No. I'm all right," he wheezed. "Don't worry about me," and he shook her hand away and stood up and pointed at their glasses and said "Want another?" He staggered and sat down again and said "Maybe not…"

"You want us to call someone?"

He shook his head. "No. But I think… I think I should just go to bed. I'm tired."

"You sure?"

"Yeah. Sure."

"Okay, but…"

"No buts, girls. You go. I'll be fine."

"We can't leave you like this."

Now he felt the prickly sensation again, this time in his head. "I paid you, yeah?"

"Yes, Harry."

"Then it's my call, right?"

"Okay. Your call."

"So go. Leave me."

"But.."

"Go!"

"Okay…"

*

The cab carrying the women met Robert Swaine's car on Hyde Hall's drive. As they met and slowed, he looked at the two women – their faces were lit by the glow of mobile phones – but then the driver pulled away and he was left alone again, his headlights illuminating the garden, the trees and the blank windows of the house.

Home. Of a sort. He'd lived there for at least ten years, maybe twelve, but it had always been just that, a place to live. A home suggested more. It suggested warmth and love and security, a place where safety was guaranteed. Was that Hyde Hall? Robert didn't think it was, and after he'd parked he sat for a minute and listened to the sound of the engine as it cooled, then climbed out, went to the front door and rang the bell. He waited a couple of minutes and then the hall light came on, latches were turned and the door opened. As it did, his father said "What did you forget…" He was wearing sweat pants, an unbuttoned sleeveless shirt and flip-flops, and when he saw his son he did a double take and took a step back and everything went swimmy.

"Dad?"

"Er.."

"Dad? What the hell's going on? You're looking terrible."

"You're…"

"I'm Robert."

"I know."

"And those women…" Robert turned and pointed down the drive.

"They're friends. They're my friends." He turned and walked down the hallway to the kitchen and said "A man's allowed his friends, isn't he?"

Robert closed the door and followed his father to the kitchen. He sniffed the air. Cheap perfume, cheap wine, socks. Some music he wished he'd forgotten years ago. A bowl of crisps.

"There are friends, Dad, and there are…" he thumbed towards the front door.

"Yeah. Well, I tell you what, Robert." He leant on the breakfast bar and gave his son a long look. "Meet a girl. Get married. Stay married to her for thirty years. Give her everything you've got and then watch… watch as she runs off with someone you take off the fucking street and give a job, some loser half your age. Then tell me what I can't do…" he swept his hand into a couple of glasses and brushed them onto the floor… "tell me what I can't do in my own house."

Robert had seen his father mad but not mad and sad and drooling.

"So mind your own business…"

"Dad, I'm sorry. This is a bad time…"

"Oh, good spot."

"I'll go. I'll come back tomorrow."

"No… no…" and now Harry's voice started to almost plead. "No. Stay. Have a drink. I'll get dressed."

"Sure?"

"Sit…"

Robert nodded. "Okay."

*

The night was warm and damp, and after a fish supper on the beach, the lovers returned to their hotel, had a drink in their room and went to bed early. As they lay they listened to each other's breathing, and watched the reflections of the street light on the ceiling, and listened to the sea as it broke along the shore. The sound of people strolling and talking, a motorcycle. A pair of cats crying at each other. She turned towards him and opened her mouth to say something, but he was asleep and making little ticking sounds.

As he slept he dreamt he was at a train station, where he was expecting to pick up a hire car. But no one had a record of his booking, and the people behind the counter twirled their pens and thought the situation was funny. Fargo didn't. He asked to see a manager but she was in a café eating lunch. He hung around for a few minutes, and told anyone who'd listen that he was going to miss an appointment with that bloke off the telly who does cooking in a garden. Eventually someone got him a cab and the dream faded, and Fargo drifted into a deeper, less confusing sleep.

Anne couldn't sleep. She tried but failed and at half past twelve she got up, stood by the window and looked out at the lights of the promenade, the bay and a coin of moonlit sea. She watched the clouds and waves and then, when she heard Fargo shift in his bed, she turned to look at him. The duvet had slipped and uncovered his back. His skin shone and his muscles were calm. He shifted again and made a snuffling sound, and she felt her heart climb in her chest, and grow and change, and then slowly change back to how it was before. She wondered at the feeling and thought do you fall in love or do you slide into it? Is it less a tumble off high rocks, more a helpful someone helping you on with your coat? That feeling as your arms slide in and it first touches your shoulders and then hangs there perfectly. That feeling of warmth and security when you do up the buttons, and the joy when you push your hands into the pockets and find a pair of gloves. "Fargo…" she whispered.

She turned and looked back towards the sea, and the moonlight faded as more clouds came, and the sea reverted to a dark skin on the world and below, on the promenade, a figure stood and stared up at her. A man, his hands in his pockets, licking his lips probably, and thinking whatever. But she didn't care. People could stand and stare and do and think whatever they wanted. She had made a choice and when she went back to bed and slipped in beside Fargo, she put a hand on his shoulder and felt his slow breathing, and he stirred and said "Hey".

"Sorry," she said. "Go back to sleep."

"Okay."

The smell of tar, the taste of salt, the tug of a filling sail against the wind, the slap of a hull against skin, the sound of satisfied lips, the first note of an easy song. All these things came to Anne in the late Aberystwyth night and as she coasted towards sleep she felt as sure as that night and its morning, and as sure as the night to come.

*

Harry and Robert talked late and dark. The things they said tumbled out without much thought, drunk words between a father and son who'd never understood each other, and never even tried. The one, content to go large and build an empire of sausages, the other, anxious to acquire power and money and status and a flat with a view of the river. The one, unable to say what the other did for a living, the other unable to understand why his father rolled his sleeves up to work.

Had it always been like this? Yes, it had. This is what life is like when change is ignored. Harry saw fatherhood as something to be tolerated, an inevitable consequence of success. It wasn't something you took lightly but it wasn't something you carried, so when Robert said "Why were you never around?" he snapped back with "What are you talking about?"

"When we were kids."

"I was around. I was always around. I was there…"

"No you weren't. Out the house before we were up, back after we'd gone to bed. Some weeks we didn't see you at all."

"I was working, Robert. Providing. Providing for you and… your brother. And building. Making something, doing what I had to do…" He reached out, his hand hovered over his son's thigh, he pulled it back. "You understand that. You know. You're like me."

"I'm nothing like you, Dad."

"You're exactly like me."

170

"Yeah right…"

Harry leant back and spilt his drink. "Why do you live?"

"What?"

"Why?' He opened his arms. "Why? What for?"

"I live… I live to…"

"To make money, Robert. That's why you live. What other reason is there?"

"I dunno."

"Then that's it. To make money…" he held up his glass, "and to get drunk."

"I like to drink."

"I like to get drunk."

"Me too."

"Then drink, boy…" and he waved his hand in the direction of the ranked bottles. "Help yourself…"

"Thanks."

"Fill your boots…"

"I will…"

They drank in silence for five minutes, the silence freighted with the shared but unspoken thought that they needed to talk about something serious, but the more that thought loomed, the more it faded. So by the time a clock chimed midnight, they'd both decided that some things could wait for the morning and two plates of bacon and eggs.

*

EVERY… magazine ran the story in their edition published August 2, 2012. Under the headline KIDNAP FURY OF THE SMOKING LOVERS, the copy was halfway down the pecking order, sandwiched between BULLIED CANCER BOY'S HEARTWARMING CAKE SURPRISE and MY BABY LOOKS LIKE MUSSOLINI.

Anne Swaine, 55, runaway wife of Kent butcher Harry Swaine, looks pleased with herself, and maybe she is.

Friends say that she's kidnapped her husband's 20-year-old toy-boy gardener, and is forcing him to satisfy her every need.

True or not? We'll leave that for you to decide. But as our exclusive photos show, she's certainly got a spring in her step!

Currently enjoying the high life at a swanky hotel in Aberystwyth, North Wales, they're protected by Radar, their fearsome guard dog.

They've been blazing a lustful trail through the country, and wherever they go their smoking hot relationship gets tongues wagging, while Mrs Swaine's furious husband is said to be prepared to do anything to get her back.

As the creator of a range of award-winning sausages, does that mean he'd be prepared to give EVERY... magazine the recipe?

Let's hope so! Because if foodies in his home town of Broadstairs, Kent are to be believed, his bangers are bound to satisfy!

The story was accompanied by a selection of photographs. One showed them walking on the promenade, holding hands and smiling at the sea The next showed them sitting at a table at the café on Constitution Hill. He was staring at his mobile, she was staring at the sky. A couple of cropped head shots showed them strolling on the hill, and another was a close-up of Radar with the caption "*You wouldn't want to tangle with this bruiser.*" The final shot showed them standing outside their hotel. He was pointing at something, she wasn't looking and Radar looked like he could do with a snooze.

*

Harry and Robert never had the conversation they were going to have, the serious one that would start over breakfast and continue through the morning to coffee and dissolve over lunch, then stay quiet during the afternoon before being revived by alcohol and the evening. The one that started with cosy reminiscences about childhood days when they might have been poor but they were happy, and what had happened and what – eventually expressed – was she thinking, taking off with a kid? Was she trying to find that happiness herself, that lost place? I mean, how selfish can you be? How thoughtless? No. The two men never had that conversation because at half past nine, Robert got a call from his office.

"Robert?"

"Yeah?"

"This is Jess, at the office."

His heart sank. "Yeah Jess, what's up?" He knew. A deal was going down, he was missed and the top floor wanted to know where he was.

"Your Dad, he's a butcher, right?"

"Yeah. Why."

"In Kent? And your Mum, she's called Anne?"

"What's this about, Jess?"

"You seen EVERY?

"Every what?"

"The magazine."

"Jess. Do I look like I'm the sort of person who reads that sort of shit."

"No. But…"

"But what?"

"Your Mum's in it. With… with some kid…"

"What?"

"In some place in Wales."

"You're kidding."

"See for yourself. It's online. You can..." but Jess didn't finish what she was going to say. Robert booted his laptop and two minutes later was reading "Friends say that she's kidnapped her husband's toy-boy gardener, and is forcing him to satisfy her every need..." He called up the stairs. "Dad!"

"What?"

"Get down here."

*

Harry's car purred and as the man listened, he knew the engine knew, the wheels understood and the switches were wise. He was angry that someone had talked and now everyone knew that he couldn't control his wife, but one thing at a time. He'd get her back first, put Fargo in hospital, abandon the dog by the side of a Welsh road, and then ask questions.

His sat-nav told him that if he drove nonstop he could be in Aberystwyth by half four, but he'd need lunch so he reckoned half five. Maybe six. No later than half six. But it didn't matter. In fact, he considered, if he aimed for half seven and he was lucky, he could catch them in a restaurant. That would be ideal. So he drove steadily and enjoyed the feel of the road and when he stopped for a cup of coffee and a doughnut, he didn't rush. He drank slowly and allowed the noise and chatter to swill around him. He could taste success, and it tasted of iron and blood and sugar, and the dust of lovely threats.

His phone buzzed. Robert. The good son had left before him, driving back to London with the words "Give him a kicking from me." Now he texted "I'm home. Drive carefully, Dad. Let me know..." and for the first time in a dozen or more years, he felt proud of his boy, and wished him pleasure.

*

Anne was in the shower and Fargo was lying on the bed watching *GOOD MORNING BRITAIN* when Wells called and said "Hey, who's my bad bro. My very bad bro. I don't believe it. You should be ashamed of yourself." She laughed. "Spanked bottom for naughty Fargo…"

"What you talking about?"

"Oh come on. Don't give me that."

"Don't give you what?"

"Yeah, right. Like you don't know."

"So tell me…"

"Haven't you seen it?"

"Seen what? I'm watching telly."

"EVERY… magazine."

"No. You know I don't read that sort of crap."

"You're in it. Pictures and everything. You and your…" and she laughed again… "your girlfriend."

"What you talking about?"

"Yup. Your and her, strolling along the front in Aber… Aber…"

Now Fargo sat up. "Aberystwyth."

"That's the one. You don't look very happy. And nor does the dog. I would have thought you'd be over the moon. A woman like that. Looks like she knows one end of a stick from the other…"

"Jesus…"

"He's not going to help you…"

"What do they say?"

She started to read the copy.

"Where did they get this crap?"

"God knows."

"Okay. Ta…"

"So what are you going to…" but she didn't get a chance to finish what she was saying. Fargo hung up, jumped off the bed and banged on the bathroom door.

"Yes!"

He opened the door.

"Come to wash my back?"

"No. We have to go…"

"Go? But…"

"Now."

"Why?"

"We're in some magazine. Pictures and everything…"

"What?"

"Yes", and he told her what Wells had told him, and half an hour later they were back in the car, heading up the road towards Machynlleth. They stopped at a garage for petrol, a packet of custard creams and a copy of EVERY… magazine, and even though Anne saw the funny side of things, and laughed at every line, and said "How do they make this stuff up?" half a dozen times, Fargo reminded her that there was nothing funny about what those lies could do.

*

Other people were reading EVERY… magazine, and the features editor at the magazine's red top stable mate had already added the line *SMOKING KIDNAP LOVERS* to a list of possible stories to chase. An hour later, at the daily editorial meeting, a story about the local councillor who'd used taxpayers' money to remodel his spare bedroom as a faithful reproduction of the bridge of the USS Enterprise was dropped – "he's going down and the story's going nowhere…" – and a decision had been made.

It followed a well-trodden route – the magazine's picture editor was called, and ten minutes later, all available photos were

176

being discussed by the red top's equivalent, and half a dozen headlines were written.

"Why are they the smoking lovers?" asked a deputy editor. "I don't see them smoking?"

"Smoking hot, Eric."

"It's a bit tenuous."

"Tenuous is hot."

"Is it?"

"Who cares?"

"I think we should."

"Do you?"

"Yes."

"Then I think you're in the wrong job."

"And what does that mean?"

"Joke, love, joke."

"Don't call me love, Eric."

"Sorry."

"And you call that a joke?"

"I do."

*

A hack called Tim Joyce sat at his screen and typed *RUNNIN', LOVIN' AND SMOKIN'...* into the headline box. He stared at the words, rolled his eyes, took a deep breath, poked his tongue out of the corner of his mouth and wrote:

"Our sister title EVERY... magazine was first to pick up on the story of odd couple lovers Fargo Hawkins, 20 and Anne Swaine, 55, who are on the run from his boss and her husband. Who just happens to be the same man! A source close to well-known butcher Harry Swaine of Broadstairs, Kent say he is heart-broken and ready to do just about anything to get her back.

"They were such a happy, loving couple. A real family – it's come as a huge shock to everyone in town. It's really not the sort of thing that happens in Thanet."

Last spotted in the Welsh seaside town of Aberystwyth, and travelling with a fierce guard dog called Radar, the couple are believed to be heading north in a battered green Toyota Corolla.

Our source adds: "The first thing Harry wants is to know that Anne's safe and well. He really hasn't got a beef with Fargo..." So let us know if you spot the smokin' lovers – our news desk is waiting for your call!"

Tim thought about writing some more but he was over the 170 word limit and besides, he wasn't a happy man. He was a pale and sick and wounded and grim and grey and gloomed man. His girlfriend had dumped him, his stomach felt like it was full of rocks, his eyes were red and he had a killer headache. He had recurring dreams about turtles and he'd had a cough for a couple of weeks, and when he put all these things together and folded them into something that looked like a hammer, he knew he had cancer. And not just a simple cancer that would respond to chemo and a four minute slot on local TV news, but something angry and virulent. Something with power and greed that was ready to rip the throat out of his neck and spit it at a window. Gob sliding, glass glistening, rankling with a desperate, frantic feeling. But. But at least. But at least I can. But at least I can write, he thought, and he took a deep breath that caught at the back of his throat and almost strangled him. He was turning into a novel. An hour later his copy was dropped into page seven of the morning edition.

*

At around eight o'clock, as the sun dipped into the west and the pubs started to fill with the confused, the ragged and gangs of

damp holidaymakers, Harry pulled his Merc into an Aberystwyth hotel car park, turned the engine off and sat for a couple of
minutes. He closed his eyes. He'd made good time and although
he was feeling vaguely nauseous and lightheaded, his mind was
clear. He sat and listened as the engine ticked and cooled, then
opened his eyes and stared at the wall in front of him. It was red
and running with water, and covered in black streaks. He wondered if this meant anything but decided it didn't. So he climbed
out of the car, checked into the hotel, dumped his bags in the
room, washed his face and hands and went to find a drink.

As he stood at the bar with his first pint of the evening, he felt
the alcohol hit and allowed himself a small smile. So he didn't
know what good he was doing or how much luck he'd have
finding them, and they were probably on the road already, but he
was closer to them than he'd been in Kent, and once people like
EVERY... magazine got hold of a story they didn't let go. They'd
be his eyes and ears, all he had to do was check their online
edition every day. So when another drinker came and stood next
to him and said "Good evening," Harry said "Yes, it is, isn't it?"

"On holiday?"

"You could say that."

"You're not from round here."

"No, I'm not."

"Come far?"

Harry looked at the stranger and wondered. Why do people
insist on being idiots? Why can't they help themselves? Do they
ever think they'd be better for changing? And if they changed,
and their stupidity was modified to become something grand,
would they wonder at what they left behind and regret the waste?
"Yes," said Harry. "I have." And before the other drinker had a
chance to ask if he'd come in on the A487 or the A44, he picked

up his pint, went to a table in the corner, sat down and checked his messages.

*

Sixty miles away, Anne checked her own messages while she and Fargo walked Radar around Porthmadog harbour. Boats swung at their moorings, gulls cried and on the far side of the water, a steam engine wheezed and smoked. A coach stalled and someone yelled from an attic window. When the dog had done his business, they walked back to their hotel, an old place on the High Street with a shady patio where they sat at a table and drank under a plum tree.

"Remember that place I told you about?" said Fargo. "That place where I went on holiday when I was a kid?"

"I do. What was it called?"

"Criccieth. It's up the road. We can go there tomorrow. We can go there now…"

"Tomorrow," she said, but she wasn't thinking about where they were going next.

"You okay?"

She shook her head.

"What's the matter?"

She ran her finger around the rim of her glass, sipped her drink and sighed. "It's always going to be like this, isn't it?"

"Like what?"

"You know."

"No I don't. Tell me."

"We're always going to be running. If not from Harry, then from some newspaper or gossip mag. And if not from them, it'll be someone else."

"No it won't…"

"It's never going to stop."

"It will."

"When?"

"Soon. That mag – they'll be get bored with us by tomorrow. They'll just move on to someone else."

"You think so?"

"Of course."

"But…"

"But what? We can do this, Miss Carter. Really. We can."

"I don't know…"

"Okay." He took a long pull from his pint. "So you leave. You go home. What's going to be waiting for you?"

She shook her head.

"I'll tell you what. His fists, for a start. And then… then you're going to spend the rest of your life in misery, doing what you're told, tidying up after him, cooking his sausages?"

"I know, I know… but we haven't got any plans. Not real plans. What did we say in Aberystwyth?"

"I don't know. We said a lot of things in Aberystwyth."

"We can't live on air, Fargo. You, me. We're going to run out of money. We have to be practical. We need a place to live, work, all that…"

"Okay." He finished his pint and said "Tomorrow. Tomorrow I get a job and we find a place to live."

"As easy as that?"

"Of course." He stood up. "Want another?"

She looked at her glass and nodded.

"Same again?"

"Thanks."

*

The ad in the Daily Post read: "*GROUNDS MAINTENANCE WORKER required for busy Llyn static caravan and chalet park. Full time permanent position with immediate start. Experience in similar role preferred, and full driving licence essential as you'll be expected to drive our work vans. Live on site and must be prepared to work overtime during the season.*"

They were sitting in the hotel lounge. Fargo showed Anne the ad, said "Give me a minute…" went outside and called the number. Five minutes later he came back and said "They want to see me this morning."

"This morning?"

"Yeah. Half eleven. The last bloke left without telling anyone – they're desperate."

"Where is it?"

"Up the coast. It's outside a place called…" he ran his finger down the paper, "Abersoch." He leaned towards her and took her hand and the smile would not leave his face. "This was meant." He slapped his thighs. "It's just too right."

"Don't say that until you've seen the place."

"Okay," he said. "But…"

She leant towards him and kissed his cheek. "I suppose you should have a suit. We could buy one…"

"What for?"

"You're having a job interview, Fargo. You've got to look smart."

"I'll brush my hair, but I don't think I'll need a suit."

"It's okay," she said, as a man on the far side of the lounge put down his newspaper and stepped outside, "I was only kidding."

*

After a breakfast of four rashers of bacon, three sausages, two eggs, baked beans, mushrooms, tomato, fried bread, toast and three cups of tea, Harry went to find the hotel his wife had stayed in. It wasn't difficult. The place was four doors down from his. He stood outside it, stared at the blank windows, went inside and although he knew the answers before they came, asked the receptionist "Is a Mrs Swaine staying here? She's with a dog. A dog and a... boy."

"No. Sorry. They checked out." She flicked the register. "Yeah. Yesterday."

"Any idea where they went?"

"No. They didn't say."

"Okay. Thanks." And he went to look at the town's butcher's shops.

*

The caravan and chalet park was on a wooded hill with views of the sea and the coast that stretched from Harlech to Barmouth. Fargo dropped Anne off at the gate. "Good luck," she said, and Fargo said "How's my hair?"

"Lovely," she said, and she headed down a wooded lane to walk Radar along a beach.

The site owner was a small man with a smile and a firm handshake. "Tom," he said. "Thanks for coming."

"I'm Fargo," said Fargo.

"Unusual name."

"I know."

Tom wasn't stupid. He let the subject lie, felt the hand, let it go and got to business. Once it was established that Fargo had worked for Thanet District Council's parks department, and his ex-boss would provide a reference and he knew how to clean a rake, the deal was almost done. "Most of the work here involves mowing. Mowing, cutting, blowing. We've got a couple of Mountfield lawn tractors. You've used them?"

"Something similar. Hayters."

"Want to show me?"

"Sure."

They went outside and walked through the site to a large wooden shed. There were bins there, and a compost heap. One of the tractors was parked outside.

"There you go," said Tom. "She's all yours."

It was a newer model than any he'd driven, but the controls were familiar enough, and a minute later Fargo was steering towards a patch of grass between two caravans. He engaged the blades, dropped the cutter deck, and started mowing.

The skills came back, smooth, easy and comfortable. He went up, came back, adjusted the deck as he passed over some paving and made a careful sweep around a rotary clothes line. When he'd finished the job, he parked by the shed, turned off the tractor and said "Okay?"

Tom nodded. "We strim the steps, the edges and around the trees."

"Okay."

"And there's plenty of weeding, some litter picking."

"Sure."

"And you'd be happy to work overtime? This time of year it gets extra busy."

"No problem."

"And you've got a clean licence? If you need to pick up any equipment, parts, whatever, you'll use a pick-up."

"Clean as a whistle."

"And in the winter, there's a lot of general maintenance to do. Painting and decorating, stuff on the vans…"

"No problem. I've done that."

Tom looked at Fargo and nodded. "Okay," he said. "Job's yours if you want it. Can you start tomorrow?"

"No problem."

"Great. So. Any questions?"

"The ad did say I could live on site…"

"Yup. There's a van at the top of the site. Not sure what sort of state Joe left it in, but that's where you'll stay. Where do you live at the moment?"

"We're staying in Porthmadog."

"Me and my girlfriend."

"Okay… Got to give your present accommodation notice?"

"Not really."

"So want to see the van?"

"Yeah."

It was on its own away from the rest of the site, tucked behind a low hedge, and was in a poor state. Dirty plates in the sink, mouldering takeaway boxes on the stained carpet, a manky shower, abandoned clothes on the unmade bed. The place smelled of mould, and flies buzzed between the smeared windows and the ragged curtains. Tom shook his head. "Joe… he was a bastard. If I…" He stopped himself and took a deep breath. "Okay. We'll get this sorted. Might take a day or two, but once it's fixed it's yours if you want it."

"Sure. I mean, I'll fix it tomorrow if you want. Make it my first job."

Tom thought about that. "I wanted you to mow the bottom plots in the morning, but if you want, yeah. Spend the afternoon up here. You can pick cleaning stuff up from the store. That's down by the shop, you know, where you came in."

"Cool."

"And your girlfriend's going to be living with you?"

"If that's okay?"

Tom shrugged. "As long as she's not a wild one, I don't see why not."

Fargo laughed. "No. She's very quiet. And we've got a dog."

"A dog?"

"Yeah."

"What sort?"

Fargo shrugged. "I'm not sure."

"Well behaved?"

"Good as gold."

"Okay." Tom offered Fargo his hand. "Tomorrow. 8 o'clock."

"I'll be here."

"Good lad."

*

Fargo was happy, Anne was thoughtful, Radar wanted a bone, a stick and a snooze. They celebrated in Criccieth with ice cream and a walk along the beach. Gulls circled, kids ran towards the sea, stopped, jumped, ran back. Men stretched out and snoozed, women struggled with towels and their swimming costumes, the sun winked off the windows of a train as it trundled down the line. Behind them, high on a bluff, the ruined castle watched over the scene, flags flying from its towers, ghosts watching from the arrow slits. "This place hasn't changed," said Fargo. "And now we're going to be able to visit whenever we want."

"Did you tell him about me?"

"Yes, and Radar."

"What did he say?"

"He's cool. More than cool. As long as I do the hours, he'll be happy." The ice cream was good. "And you could live in a caravan?"

"I don't see why not. We've been living in hotel rooms…"

"But after Hyde Hall, it's going to be small."

"Hyde was always too big. It didn't matter how much you turned the heating up, it was always cold. And you could never find anything, or anyone. But most of all, and this was the worst thing, it was lonely." She reached out and took his hand. "Very lonely. I'm going to be very happy in a caravan." She let his hand go, reached up, stroked his face and stared at the waves. "And happy with you. Believe me."

"I do," he said.

"But you've got to understand – this is the first time in years, decades, that I've done something for myself, made a decision that didn't have something to do with what to have for dinner or whether to vacuum the stairs today or tomorrow. Have you any idea how difficult that is for someone like me? I look at you and remember how I was when I was your age."

"And?"

"When I could do something without thinking of the consequences."

"I think of the consequences all the time."

"Okay. Maybe you do, but the older you get, the more you let your head do the thinking. Your heart… your heart gets stiff. You forget how to be brave. How to take a chance."

"Your heart can get stiff, Miss Carter. And you can forget to be brave. That is, some people can. You haven't."

"You think so?"

He laughed. "You're the bravest person I know."

"Oh please."

"You are. Brave and fabulous."

"I'm that?"

"And more."

"Tell me."

"Later," he said, and he slipped his arm around her waist and felt her flesh and she slipped her arm around his and they stopped by a breakwater, leaned back and kissed, and it started to rain.

*

The rain started as fat single drops, dotting the sand and rocks, but then the sky split and boomed, and the shower turned to a downpour. People ran for cover, kids squealed, cafés filled. Anne and Fargo and Radar didn't care. They walked back to the car and drove back to Porthmadog slowly. Contentment was in the air, and ease.

They weren't expecting the sudden or the stupid, so as they walked from the car to the hotel, they didn't notice the photographer on the other side of the road. He was parked in his own car, laptop on the passenger seat, lens propped on the edge of the open window. He took eighteen shots, checked the quality, chose six, and two minutes later they were dropping into the inbox of the picture editor at EVERY... magazine's red top sister. Half an hour later, Tim Joyce, now more depressed than he'd ever been in his life, now feeling the rocks in his stomach actually were rocks, wrote up the story thus: YOU FIND THE SMOKIN' LOVERS!

Our readers never let us down. When we ask you to help us out, you always come up with the goods! So when we asked you to let us know if you'd seen the Smokin' Lovers, we knew you wouldn't let us down. An eagle-eyed reader spotted them in the Welsh town of Porthmadog and as you can see, they're still happy to do what comes naturally. And what comes naturally to this pair comes very naturally. So what next for the love-crazed odd couple? Watch this space...

*

And the night came down over all the people, a smoky blanket pulled itself over a sleepy world, and the birds were quiet in their roosts. Foxes climbed cars and lay down to warm their bellies. Cows were quiet. Cats stalked. Painters worried, writers botched, singers felt the catch in their throats, nurses drifted into their dreams, a doctor took his last call. Someone backed their car into a garage, turned off the engine and sat for a moment in the quiet, and stared at a wall.

In Aberystwyth, Harry lay in a bed that was too small for him, his belly full of beer and curry, his head aching and his heart racing. His face was covered in a mask of sweat, and when he closed his eyes, spots of light swam in the dark. His breathing was too fast and he felt a vague sense of unease, as though eyes were watching him, but he didn't know where they were. Maybe they were in the smoke detector that blinked on the ceiling, or perhaps in the wardrobe. The wardrobe was cheap and its door didn't close properly. There was a crack that eyes could peep from, red and staring eyes, a wounding look, maybe even a killing one. He turned over and lay so he could watch the street light against the curtains. The shadows of raindrops ran against the light, and the sound of waves. A car raced beneath the window, then another, and a motorbike.

In London, Robert was working late, sitting on a stool in his kitchen with a laptop on the counter. He was calculating the CAPEX on the refurb of three oil rigs and an accommodation platform. A television was on with the sound down – he'd watched the end of *NEWSNIGHT* and now he was keeping an eye on a programme about the Welsh in Patagonia. He stopped working to focus on a sequence that featured a pair of farmers riding their horses across a field. The camera rose and panned and swept and the image was picked up by a drone and the landscape opened and filled, and a minute later the horses and riders were tiny dots in an wilderness of grass and sky and wind. In the distance, mountains rose, or were they an optical illusion, and lakes? Robert squinted at the screen and wondered. He turned up the volume and music was playing to accompany the scene, a piece of lilting major key jazz. A fat tenor sax, big piano, upright bass, strapped drums. The music was beautiful and the scene so lovely that he suddenly felt himself welling up. A lump came to his throat and his eyes narrowed, he gulped for air and then he started to weep, great heaving sobs and sighs. And once he started he couldn't stop and a flood came, and there was nothing he could do to stop it. Gasping and choking, he grabbed a handful of paper towels, and held them to his face. He closed his eyes and tried to take a deep breath but only managed to make a noise like a train braking – a terrible squealing that came from deep in his belly. He tried to blow his nose but gagged. He stood up, staggered to the bathroom and ran a tap. He splashed cold water on his face for a minute, then straightened and stared at himself in the mirror. "What the fuck..." he said to himself.

Three miles away, in another part of the city, the hack Tim Joyce lay on a sofa in a basement flat and listened to his upstairs neighbours make love. He couldn't avoid this. She was a screamer, he was a pounder, the ceiling was thin and the light bulb swayed. But he wasn't enjoying the performance. The rocks in his stomach were heavier than they'd ever been and had pinned him to the sofa, and he couldn't move a single muscle in his body. Not even his lips.

And in Porthmadog, Anne lay on her stomach and Fargo traced a line from her neck, down her spine to her waist. They'd made love and now, as they drank a bottle of wine, the light reflected off Anne's cheeks with a glow that reminded him of cheese. And when he thought of cheese he grew hungry. His stomach rumbled and he said "Are you hungry?"

"Yes."

"Fancy something?"

She lifted her head and smiled. "Asking or offering?"

He laughed.

She turned towards him and lifted her face. He kissed the tip of her nose. "What time is it?"

"Ten."

"Fancy a take away?"

"Fish and chips?"

"Why not?"

"But then bed. I can't be late on my first day."

"You won't be."

Half an hour later Fargo was standing in a queue of hungry late boys in a warm place called PETE'S PLAICE. Anne was outside with Radar. He bought two small cod and chips and they walked down to the harbour, sat on a bench and ate. The warmth of the food through the paper, the lovely smell, the sound of the batter's crunch, the look of the white flesh, the pleading in Radar's eyes, the gentle clack of rigging, the drizzle curtaining though the orange light of the street lamps – these things combined to create an atmosphere of satisfaction and contentment, as if any change would be pointless because the changes already made were perfect and complete, and nothing was lost.

*

Morning. London. One of Robert Swaine's colleagues dropped a newspaper on his desk, open at the page that featured two shots of his mother and Fargo walking down a street in Porthmadog. He scanned the copy, called his father, and told him everything

KIDNAP FURY OF THE SMOKING LOVERS

he needed to know. The name of the street, the name of the hotel, the colour of his mother's trousers.

"Thanks, Rob. I owe you."

"Where are you now?"

"Aberystwyth."

"Where's that?"

"Where do you think?" and ten minutes later he was driving north.

*

Seventy-five miles away, Fargo had already been at work for an hour, and had already impressed his boss by fixing a broken strimmer. There'd been a double take when Anne stepped out of the car but it hadn't lasted more than a second. Fargo had been right. Tom was more than cool. As long as people did what they were supposed to do and didn't take off without giving notice, he was happy. So when someone in the site office showed him a copy of a paper with shots of his new gardener walking down the street in Porthmadog, he shrugged and said "His personal life is just that. If he puts the hours in, I don't care. And from what I've seen, he's a grafter. So you can take this..." and he picked up the paper, folded it, and dropped it in a bin "...and stick it."

Anne spent the morning in the caravan, cleaning, washing and filling bin bags with rubbish. Then she sat at the table by the big window and made a list of things they needed. Sheets, towels, toiletries, knives and forks, plates and mugs, other stuff for the kitchen. She showed the list to Tom and asked him where the best shops were – he said "Pwllheli or Porthmadog. Either..."

"Thanks."

"No worries."

"Anything you'd like me to pick up for yourself?"

"No ta."

*

Harry arrived in Porthmadog at half past ten, found the hotel and asked the owner – the widow Mrs Cynthia Kelman, originally of Liverpool but settled now in Wales – what room the middle-aged woman, the boy and the dog were in. He got the answer he was half expecting and didn't expect any joy when he asked if she knew where they were now. So when she said "I do" he spluttered "You do?"

"Yes. And I suppose…" she said, tapping a copy of the newspaper on the desk, "you want to know."

"I do."

A smile sneaked her face, made her lips quiver and forced her head sideways. "I heard them talking last night."

"And?"

"He got himself a job."

"Where?"

"Abersoch. On a caravan site."

"And where's that?"

"Down the coast. About twenty minutes. Maybe half an hour."

"Twenty minutes?"

"Yes."

"You…" he said, and he put a finger to his lips, "are a diamond."

Mrs Kelman had never been called a diamond before, not even when Mr Kelman had been alive, for he had only ever grimaced and said things like "If I hadn't have met you I could have…" and "Why don't you wear something different for a change?" and "Cook it." So she blushed and as the blood raced to her cheeks, her fingers tingled. And when Harry saw her blush, he was suddenly infested with his own feelings. These swept from hot to cold and back to hot again, and he wondered if her colour had anything to do with him, or if she was just feeling flushed. And as he thought these things, he suddenly felt more than odd and had to grab the counter to steady himself.

"Are you all right?" said Mrs Kelman, and put her hand on his arm.

"I think..." he said. "I'm feeling..." and he staggered backwards, saw a chair, felt for it and collapsed.

"Oh my," said Mrs Kelman, and she rushed to get a glass of water.

When she got back, Harry was slumped and panting, and his face was the colour of raw bacon. She said "I think you need a doctor..."

"No. No doctors." He took the water and drank. "No. All I need is to sit down for a minute." He drank some more, and gulped for breath.

"Are you sure? You look terrible."

"I'll be fine. Really. Thank you."

She put a hand on his arm and then felt his forehead. "But you're burning up."

He smiled now. Her hand was so cool and her voice so calm, and when he looked into her eyes he saw something but couldn't think of the word to describe it. Tranquillity? Maybe. Like a cool lake. Serenity? Could be. A view of heaven from the back of a camel? Yes. "Could I have another glass of water?"

"Of course," she said, and she took the empty glass from his hand and went to refill it.

And as he watched her go, something switched in his head, and instead of watching the spreading arse of a widowed hotel manager retreat towards the door of a dingy kitchen, he watched an angel float on a small cloud of love, her perfect wings folded against the small of her back, and the door she pushed was fashioned from sheets of lacquered sandalwood. The smell of frankincense drifted in the air, and the sound of bells tinkled. And when, two minutes later, she returned, her face was glowing with compassion, her eyes fired with care, and her hands were soft perfection. She handed him the glass and smiled, and her teeth rang with tunes.

"Thank you," he said, and he thought his voice sounded different.

'You're welcome," she said.

And he drank, and the water tasted of snow or swans, and he felt a lot better. And as he swallowed another mouthful, the clouds opened and a shaft of light streamed in through the stained glass half-light at the top of the hotel front door, and colour flooded the world. Colour and silence, and the border of peace.

*

Anne cruised the shops of Pwllheli, bought the things she needed and then found a café where she sat with a cup of tea and a piece of cake.

People came and went, the air bubbled with gossip and chat, the air steamed, the air tasted of life and friendship. The windows streamed and every time the door opened, some new name was called. A woman nursed a child, the child sucked and snuffled, a man came and ordered a pie to take away, another woman came and sat beside the nursing mother, smiled and touched the top of the baby's head.

Anne's cake was a Victoria sponge, light and fluffy and filled with strawberry jam. The tea was strong. Here – she thought – in places like this, life has the power to forget pain, become its own reason and be exactly what it should be. And this – she thought – is the sort of place where even the meanest living soul could feel a lightening, and the poorest pocket would fill with riches. And when a waitress came over and asked her if she wanted some more tea, she said "Yes, please," and she thought yes, into every life will come deliverance.

*

Harry lay in bed. He'd checked into the Porthmadog hotel, and Mrs Kelman had told him that if he didn't phone for a doctor then she would. So now, Dr Trollope, an elderly GP with a rough beard and enormous eyes, checked his blood pressure, his heartbeat, the condition of his skin and the colour of his eyes. "And what's your profession?"

"I'm a butcher."

Dr Trollope smiled and nodded. "I'd have put money on that."

"Why?"

"So you eat plenty of meat? Bacon, sausages…"

"Of course."

"Smoke?"

"Sometimes."

"And how often is sometimes?"

"Ten a day."

"So that's twenty."

Harry looked at his hands.

"Drink?"

Harry nodded.

"Units?"

"I don't know."

"Pints then…"

"Half a dozen. A few shorts. The normal."

"Half a dozen pints and a few shorts is not normal," and Dr Trollope folded his stethoscope and stood up to his full height.

"I can't relax without a drink and a smoke, and if I can't relax..."

Dr Trollope held up his hand, palm front, traffic stopping. "You've just had a minor heart attack, and just avoided something worse. A lot worse." He opened his bag and dropped the stethoscope inside. "You want my advice, Mr Swaine?"

"Do I have any choice?"

"Cut out the fags. Stop drinking. Change your diet. Fruit and veg, less sausages."

"My sausages are award winning."

"I couldn't care if your sausages shoot from the arse of a Greek god whistling 'Ave Maria'. If you don't make some changes, the next doctor you see... actually change that. The next doctor you won't see will be performing your post-mortem." He picked up his bag. "Apologies for the rather brusque bedside manner, but sometimes needs must. I think these days it's known as 'tough love'. You can complain all you want to the GMC, but I'm retiring in three weeks, so frankly, I don't give a damn what you do."

"I've been under a lot of stress."

Dr Trollope shook his head. "And everyone else has been at the fairy queen's ball?"

"My wife ran off with the gardener."

"You want a competition in grief?"

"What do you mean?"

"My wife was killed by a drunk driver. Knocked down on a zebra crossing. He got 18 months. She got a box and 1800 degrees."

Harry had primed something else to say, but now all he could manage was "I'm sorry". And as the words came and the doctor said "Take my advice, Mr Swaine. Cut down on just about everything you do…" Harry realised that he probably had never heard those words, not ever in fifty-nine years of bloated life, and they did not sound like chimes.

*

After the doctor had left, Mrs Kelman came to see Harry, stood at the foot of the bed and said "Well? What did he say?"

He raised a hand and said "You were right."

"About what?"

"Everything."

She nodded and said "And I get the feeling that you're not in the habit of listening. Or doing what's best for yourself."

"You might be right about that too. I don't know."

"I am."

"You are."

"So…" she said, but not in a cruel way, "You're going to spend the rest of the day in bed, and you only get up if you're going to the bathroom." She smiled. "And you'll have some soup for your lunch. Something healthy."

"Soup?"

"Yes. Tomato soup and some crackers."

"I haven't had tomato soup for ages."

"Then it'll be a nice change for you."

"If you say so."

"I do." She stepped around the bed, hesitated for a moment and then laid a hand on his arm. Her skin was warm and soft, and when she said "Now rest, Harry. Try and get some sleep," his chest tightened, and a pain shot from his left shoulder, down the side of his body and stabbed him in the waist. But then, as quickly as this pain had come it was gone, and he felt a peace come down. And with this peace came wonder, and questions. What is happening? Where am I going? Why am I allowing a woman to tell me what to do? He closed his eyes and listened to her feet as she moved away from the bed. Then she said "Sleep…" and the word sounded like a bell and she opened the door, and the squeak of the hinges came to him like the sound of bird song in a shaded wood, with leaves turning in the air and settling on all trouble.

*

Anne spent her afternoon arranging cups and saucers, plates and knives and forks, cleaning windows and making the bed. She'd found some pictures in a charity shop, some cushions and half a dozen books. She'd bought some flowers, and arranged them in a vase. She sang as she worked and when she'd finished, she stood back and looked at what she'd done, and smiled. The place looked like a home, and smelled like a home. One of the pictures was of a sailing ship in a stormy sea, another was of a shaded house in a sunny town in France. Bougainvillea was growing from the house's balcony, its shutters were open, and curtains blew in a breeze.

She went to the little kitchen and made a pot of tea. She stood over the pot as the steam rose, trapped the heat with the lid, sat down at the table, took out her phone and scrolled through the numbers until she came to Mike's. She dialled, listened to the tone and when she was put through to voicemail, took a deep breath and said the words she'd rehearsed. "Hello darling. I just wanted to tell you that we're in Wales and think we've landed on our feet. Fargo's got a job with a place to live – ring me when you get this and I'll tell you more. Love you…" and she hung up and scrolled through to Robert's. This was more difficult and she knew she wasn't brave enough. She stared at his name and drifted to a memory of the day he was born. A happy, bright day in July, hot as a grill. A cosy maternity home, the sort they don't have any more. A bossy midwife, the scent of carbolic and talc, stiff sheets. A family complete and perfect, like something from a book. But what book? What story? What nonsense, what lies, what distant moaning of a train? And what trouble? "Later," she said to the floor, and went to pour her tea.

*

Harry slept and he dreamt deep and solid, and his mother came to him. She was wearing a high waisted floral dress, a cardigan and her hair was curled under a colourful scarf. She was holding a handbag and had a small hanky pushed into her sleeve. He could smell her, the scent of roses, dust and rain, and she smiled as she came towards him and said "Hello darling. How long has it been?"

He spoke in his dream. He said "Mother. I'm over here."

"I can see you," she said. "And I love you, Harry."

"Why are you here?"

"Why shouldn't I be?"

"Because you're dead, Mother."

"That's true," she said, and she smiled.

Harry's mother had died in 1997 after a short illness. He hadn't been there.

He'd been working. At the time, he hadn't thought twice but now, in the dream, he felt a regret that hardened and clogged the back of his throat. He coughed to clear the clog, but it was no use.

He watched as she turned and walked towards a door. He followed, and when she opened the door he watched as she stepped into a field, stretched out her arm and waited. The sky was blue, the sun high, the trees still and tight with leaves. A moment passed and then he saw a dot in the sky. And as the moment became a minute so the dot became a hawk, and the hawk landed on her fist. It folded its wings and as it did this, she turned her head and said "Why would someone who loves birds make a hawk wear a hood and keep it in a cage?"

"I have no idea," he said.

"Could you find out?"

"Maybe. I could try."

"Please try. Please."

"Okay Mother."

"For the hawk trusts, Harry. It trusts the man not to steal her mouse."

*

The hawk trusts the man not to steal her mouse. The mouse narrows its tiny eyes and faints. The hawk wonders and the man – now a woman – trusts the hawk to return. This is the dynamic of enslavement and one way to keep cruelty as sweet as a berry. And in the same way, the sky relies on the bleeding sun. For the sun knows nothing and dogs swim in their own blood. All this liberalism balances the scales and keeps the ego easy. And so. So it goes.

Harry spent another day in bed, and when he got up he felt light headed and unsure of his balance. He stared at his feet and wondered. Were they there or were they gone? He had to hold the banister to go downstairs, and when he reached the dining room, he fell into the nearest chair with a painful sigh. Mrs Kelman still refused to let him go out, so he spent another couple of days sitting in the hotel lounge, reading magazines and newspapers.

The story of his wife and her lover dwindled as a child loses interest in a toy; one day it was three paragraphs and one

201

picture, and by the time it was one paragraph and no picture he surprised himself by shrugging and turning the page. When it was overtaken by a story about a woman who kept her husband locked in a wardrobe and only allowed him to eat biscuits, he shook his head, resolved never to read another newspaper again, and went to look at the books on a shelf. He ran his fingers over the spines and picked ON THE BEACH by Nevil Shute.

He couldn't remember the last time he'd read a novel, but what else was there to do? Watch the television? It was nothing but rubbish. Tune into the radio? He wasn't interested in listening to people talk about the cost of flights during the school holidays. So he started to plough his way through the book and surprised himself by enjoying it, and halfway through, when one of the characters said something about marriage, he sat up with a jolt, for reading had made him forget why he was where he was, and what he was doing in Wales.

That evening, as he sat with a cup of tea and a plate of biscuits in Mrs Kelman's private lounge, he said "I'm feeling better."

"Is that for you to say?"

"I think I know what I'm feeling."

"So I suppose that means you'll be wanting to visit Abersoch."

"What?"

"To see your wife."

He sipped his tea. "My wife…"

"Yes."

"I've been thinking about her."

"Of course you have."

"And I need to phone work. They'll be wondering where I am."

"Will they?"

"Yes. I've got shops. Butcher's shops."

"You said."

"Did I?"

"Yes."

"I don't remember…"

"I'd say," said Mrs Kelman, "that there's a lot more you need to forget."

*

Anne and Fargo resolved to be calm, quiet and easy. He would mow the grass and strim the edges, she would take Radar for long walks, he would wipe his feet on the mat, she would get a job in a tea shop, he would take up whittling animals from pieces of wood he found on the beach. She would write a cookbook. It would be called TWO RING GOURMET. It would focus on the stuff she'd learnt years before, and yes she knew about trade marks and yes she knew Cordon Bleu wasn't fashionable any more and the tone of pretension had changed but what the hell. So cookbooks were all about fresh, sustainable, local ingredients and dobs of sauce that looked like seagull shit but she didn't care. She'd write it anyway. And she was going to repair and rebuild her relationships with her sons. And she wasn't going to listen to gossip or care what anyone thought about her. She wasn't being yelled at or told she was useless, and she wasn't being punched. She was being appreciated, respected and loved. So the caravan was small and smelled of mushrooms and she'd slept in a better bed but who, as they died, has regretted not having a bigger kitchen, a fatter mattress or a taller wardrobe? And who has looked at the remains of their life and wondered if they could stuff it into a bigger bag? Only a fool, and only a fool worries about the colour of a cupboard.

*

And so, on a Monday morning in early July, as fat clouds rolled and the steady rain poured, Harry Swaine thanked Mrs Kelman for breakfast and said he'd see her later. She had brown eyes and toast crumbs on her tabard, and played with her hair as she said "You shouldn't be doing this, Harry."

"I have to."

"Wait a few days. They're not going anywhere. If Dr Trollope knew what you were doing, he'd have a fit."

"Dr Trollope can go screw himself."

"Harry!"

"I'm sorry. Forgive me. I'm a rude man." He put his hand over his heart. "I always have been."

She shook her head and gave him a little smile. "Are you sure you can drive?"

He coughed. He tasted iron. "I'm fine."

"No you're not."

"I'm more than fine," he said, "and to prove it, I'll see you later. I'll have the best room in the place, okay?"

"You've got the best room..."

"Then keep it for me," he said, "and to thank you for everything, I'm going to take you out to dinner. What's the best restaurant in town?"

She told him.

"Book a table for two. Half eight?"

"Can we make it eight?"

"Why not?" he said, and he turned, climbed into his car and drove away.

He had time so he drove slowly, through the town of Criccieth and along the smooth road to Pwllheli. The big car purred and he smiled. He rang his fingers through his hair and stopped to buy a cup of coffee and drove on to find a place where he could sit to drink with a view of the shore. He liked the view. It suited his mood. Big waves, blowing sand, rain drumming on the windscreen and the roof. The windows steamed. He didn't turn on the radio. Maybe – he thought – one day I'll give up the butchering and sell the house and find a place with a balcony and a good view of the sea, and I'll find something new to do with my time.

He drove on, and when he reached Abersoch he stopped at a garage, filled his tank and asked the man behind the counter where the caravan site was.

"Which one?"

"How many are there?"

"Plenty. What's it called?"

Harry told him.

"Okay – you go back the way you came, take a left at the pizza place, up the road and you can't miss it."

"Thanks."

He had no idea what he was going to do, and when he found the site entrance he stopped and rested his hands on the steering wheel. He thought for a moment, listened to the engine and scratched his head. Surprise. That's what he wanted. It was needed. So he turned around, drove back towards the town, parked with a load of other cars outside a row of houses and then walked back to the site.

A wind was blowing, whipping the rain into swirls and eddies. It took him twenty minutes and by the time he reached the gate, he was tired and soaked and wanted a bacon sandwich. He wanted a bacon sandwich, an egg sandwich and a pasty. A mug of coffee and two doughnuts. He stopped at the shop, dripped on the carpet and rang a bell on the counter. A woman came out and asked him if he was okay. He said "Fine…" and "I'm looking for someone."

"Who?"

"He's called Fargo."

"Fargo?"

"Yes."

The woman shrugged and said "Is he a guest?"

"He works here."

"Hang on." She disappeared out the back and came back a minute later. "He's the new lad, right?"

"Yes."

"Okay. He's probably working, but you could try his van." She ripped a map of the site off a pad, and said "It's here." She marked a cross on the map. "Out of the shop, left and follow the road past the swimming pool, up the hill and it's the one on its own with the green fence. You can't miss it."

"Thanks."

"No worries."

The rain had stopped. He followed the woman's directions, and when he found the van he stopped. There was no sign of life, no car and no lights, but he went up to the door and banged with his fist. No reply. He cupped his face against one of the windows and peered in. Motes drifted, nothing else moved. He turned away. He saw a white plastic lawn chair. He picked it up and carried it to a place where he could sit in the shelter of a hedge and a line of trees. When he realised he could be seen by three other caravans, he picked it up and carried it to a place behind a low bank. Then, when he was sure he could see but not be seen, he sat down, pulled his coat tight around his chest, crossed his arms and waited.

*

Whether we plan or avoid it, we change because this is our reason, meaning and place. We might leave a comfortable house and find a place in the west in a caravan with a man we love, or we might sit in the private lounge of a Welsh hotel and wait for a plump butcher who has promised to take us out to dinner. We might decide to become a fisherman or a sheep farmer or a rally driver, and leave a secure job to do one of these things, or we might not have any sort of plan at all but go to our office in a shining tower, spray lighter fluid into the back of our computer and set fire to it. Whatever we do and however we plan it, change is the melody that plays over the rhythm of our life.

And whether we wish for them or wish them away, endings are the chords that are waiting for us, the fingers poised over the keys, the keys staring up at our poor eyes, our eyes blanking back. For death – like life – is just another place to visit. A home to be looked forward to, the place where anyone can find a comfortable chair, a place to bathe and a wide bed.

When they found Harry, he was sitting in the white plastic lawn chair, his eyes half closed and his mouth open. Given the signs, his expression should have been one of expectation but it was of resignation, tinted with surprise. Some birds had been nesting in the trees that overhung his hiding place, and his head and shoulders were spotted with their droppings. He didn't have a bag with him, and his shoes weren't muddy.

The day he was found was Fargo's day off, and he and Anne had driven to Beddgelert where they'd visited an old copper mine. They'd walked through tunnels and climbed shafts that had been dug into a mountain, stared at carefully dressed mannequins and listened to taped stories of how the miners had worked for pennies in candlelight. Later, they'd had a cup of coffee and shared a slice of chocolate cake, and stared out at a hill where a dragon used to live. The police were still working when they got back to the caravan site, and the place where

Harry had been sitting was taped off, but the investigation was winding down.

"What's been going on?" said Fargo.

"Holiday maker." A policeman pointed, closed his notebook and tucked it into his pocket.

"What happened?"

The policeman shrugged. "Can't say anything right now. Sorry…" but ten minutes later, when he went to the shop, Tom and the shop staff were buzzing with gossip.

"Old bloke, had a heart attack. They reckon he'd only been there all day. Thing is, no one recognised him and no one's missing, so he wasn't a guest."

"I reckon he was a tramp."

"Not with shoes like that. Did you see them? Good shoes."

"There was that tramp in the paper, left a million quid to a cats' home."

"He wasn't a tramp…"

"Was."

"What did he look like?" said Fargo.

"There wasn't a picture."

"No. The bloke today."

"He looked dead."

"Fat and dead."

"Fat, dead and not a tramp."

*

Two days later, when a policewoman knocked on the caravan door to tell Anne who they'd found sitting in the lawn chair, the news didn't come as a surprise. She'd already felt something lift, the dread of expectation had faded and when the woman spoke the words, she didn't feel a loss, a passing or darkness come to whisper. She simply shook her head when she was asked if she wanted someone to visit and then, after ten minutes sitting with the motes and the quiet, she walked to the beach with Radar.

As she walked, she didn't feel uneasy, watched or poor. The sand was fine, and here and there she found a perfect shell. She felt an extra lightness but not a lot more, and when she tried to count the years since she'd met him, she couldn't. Was it 34 or 35? More? Less, probably, but it felt more. And later, when Fargo came home from work and she told him what had happened, he was almost shocked when she said "And good riddance".

"He is dead though. He was a man…"

"I don't care. I'm not going to pretend that I do. Why should I? He was a bully. He made my life a misery."

He didn't have a reply to that, so he said "What are you going to do?"

"What do you mean?"

"Well. I suppose, I don't know…"

"You suppose what, Fargo?"

He shrugged, couldn't say, but he knew. He knew that now the fat man was gone she'd be gone too, heading back to her house and the things she swore she didn't miss.

"I don't."

"Yes you do."

"Prove it."

"I will. But I have to go back for a week or two."

"Of course you do."

"But I'll come back here."

"Of course you will."

Of course you will. He let these four words rattle in his head and then their echo faded. He didn't do irony, words that meant little and sounded cheap, but he couldn't help himself. Because whatever she knew now, or thought she knew, what was coming was inevitable. So he calmed himself by pouring a can of beer and sitting at the caravan window and looking out as children played on the neat patches of grass he'd mown.

Anne pulled on an apron and went to the fridge. "I bought some steak," she said. "Okay for you?"

"Great," he said, "but don't start cooking yet. I left something in the shed." He stood up and went to the door.

"What?"

"Just something," he said, and he opened the door and stepped outside.

Anne watched as he walked away, his easy walk, his swinging arms and his head. And then, thinking that she'd wait for his return, she opened a bottle of wine and poured herself a glass, and drank.

*

At the time, no one understood why a woman like Mrs Anne Swaine took off with Fargo Hawkins and drove from the town of Broadstairs in England to Abersoch in Wales, where he got a job at a caravan site and she found work in the tea shop attached to a popular art gallery where refreshments were available in a conservatory or on the lawn if it wasn't raining. No one understood, but they did end up caring because their lives were reflections of possibility and in that year, possibility had been thieved by cats, foxes and ghosts. But if ghosts are memories that cannot be quiet – and they are – then it is our task to listen to their whispers and the rustle of their gowns, and take a lesson from their marriages, their loves and their sorrows. For what is a sorrow but an altar?

The year was 2012, and as the summer spat its sweats and turned to autumn, and a few dry days came, Anne stood by Hyde Hall's front door. The funeral was over, her sons had come and gone, the sun had faded behind fat clouds and doors and curtains had been closed. There had been arguments and accusations and deep breaths but in the end tears had won the war and now the house was empty and cold, and estate agents had called. They'd stroked their chins and made notes and put a value on the place, and as Anne and her sons considered the figure, their brains had swirled. "What? That much?"

"Of course."

"Good God."

"What were you expecting?"

"Not that much."

"Broadstairs is on the up. Give it a couple of years and you'll have HS1. And then watch prices…"

"Sure, but that's mad money."

"Hang on to it for a couple more years and then you'll see mad."

"No. We're selling. Agreed?"

"Yeah."

"Okay."

"Are we sure?"

"I want shot of the place."

"I never want to see it again."

Anne said nothing.

Later, a taxi appeared. The driver stepped out and said "Mrs Swaine?"

"Yes."

"Where to?"

"The station."

The driver was cheerful and talkative. Once they were on the road he said "Going anywhere nice?"

"Oh yes," she said.

He caught her eye in the mirror and winked. "Somewhere hot?"

"Might be," she said.

"Going to tell me where?"

She smiled and mimed the action of zipping her lips, then opened the window, sat back and let the September breeze play with her hair.

*

Take the road from Abersoch. It's flat and then it climbs, not like someone who likes mountains but like someone who wants ten minutes of slope. Stop. Stop and then start again and carry on.

Head west. Look right. Ignore. Turn left. Leave your company behind and when you find a place where the roads thin and the hedges fail, park your car and walk for a few miles. Stop again.

Sit down. Wonder why you didn't pack a sandwich, an apple and a bottle of water. Think when you can, or don't. Here's a cow, there's a sheep, here's a dozing dog and a rusting tractor in a field. Its flat tyres look like skin and its paint is the colour of a robin's egg. Crack it.

Stop for the third time. Everything is pale but suddenly you can see a slice of the sea, then the sea dips behind a hill before it appears again. The dark wine, the warm gaze, a drunken choir, the echo of all the days we've lived. A tunnel of trees and a place where the road splits and if you know your way you can walk towards a spot where the land has slipped and the greyed tarmac falls towards a cliff. Trees and shrubs grow through the white lines, a farmer's caravan rocks and rusted cogs litter the fields.

And here, if you look, you'll find a small flight of stone steps, a gate in a wall and the overgrown path that leads to a poet's abandoned house.

The house is low, white and famous, and an empty glove waves from a small window. The place is being swallowed by its own ground and the road that leads to it is collapsing, and although some people remember the poet because he hated noise and vacuum cleaners, other people know that the last years of his life were no reflection of its irascible majority.

Our lovers found the place by mistake. They weren't looking for it but the gate was half open so they pushed their way into the garden and past the blue half-door where someone took a noted photograph of the poet, his body hunched and his face twisted in fury.

The garden was overgrown and the first gale of autumn had blown leaves from the trees, but they found chairs and sat for half an hour to watch the waves sweep onto the beach below. They shouldn't have been there but they let their feelings of guilt go and allowed themselves to enjoy the light afternoon.

They were a mile or more from the shore but they could hear the roar of the waves, and see surfers. Anne closed her eyes and dozed for a few minutes – she woke up comfortably and turned to look at Fargo. He wasn't in his chair. She sat up and saw him further down the garden, collecting blackberries from a hedge. "Hey," she said.

"Tonight," he called, "let's make a pie."

"Apple and blackberry?"

"Yes."

"Or a crumble? I'd make you my special crumble."

"Why's it special?"

"That's," she said, "for me to know."

"Yeah, right," he said, and he turned back to the hedge and carried on with his picking. She closed her eyes again and crossed her hands in her lap. The sun came out for a few minutes and warmed the refrain of the day, and everything became a stolen garden. A shutter clicked and in that moment we all turned, put our hands in our pockets, turned our faces to the autumn sun and closed our eyes. The last birds of the season were singing, and the roads were empty. The roads were empty and the lanes that cut the woods that surrounded the cottage were quiet. Someone called across the valley below but they didn't call for us or any of our friends, so we said goodbye, waved a hand and walked away.